NASTY BET

THE ANTI-HERO CHRONICLES

MIKA LANE

HEADLANDS PUBLISHING

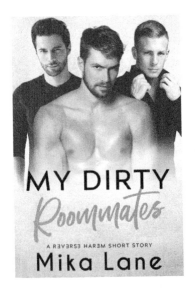

<u>My Dirty Roommates</u>

When my three sexy roommates agree to help me as long as I do whatever they ask...I can't say no.

The last thing I expect when I take a job in a new town is to end up living with three smoking hot roommates. Who also happen to be personal trainers. They are so out of my league, and I am so out of my element. But I can't afford to live alone in San Francisco, so have resigned myself to sharing.

Apparently, these guys like to share too... Overhearing them say I'm cute gives me a nice ego boost. But I want to get in shape, and they'll only help me under one condition...

I have to do *whatever* they tell me to, *whenever* they tell me to do it. Instead of scaring me, the thought of being at their beck and call sounds hot. And once they start with their naughty demands, I want them to never stop. They work me hard in the gym and everywhere else.

This whole roommate situation just put a new spin on 'sharing.'

COPYRIGHT

Like deals and other cool stuff?
Sign up for my newsletter!
https://mikalane.com/join-mailing-list/

1

LEO

"Miss, are you aware that shoplifting is a crime?"

She frowned at my hand on her arm and then at my face, her eyes widening, her lips parting, closing, then parting again.

All with no sound. Or blinking.

If she hadn't been so goddamn gorgeous, she would have reminded me of a fish gasping for air.

Other midday shoppers filtered around us without a second look, intent on their errands, and, like most New Yorkers, uninterested in anyone else's business. Even the business of blatant thievery.

Although, it was doubtful the woman who'd just slipped a very expensive evening clutch into her shopping bag had meant to be blatant, but because she was amateurish, she was also blatant. A newbie, to be sure.

Which I found all the more intriguing.

"And, if shoplifting is a crime, then I believe that makes you a criminal."

This was fun.

Yeah, I was a dick.

"Uh… um… I…"

Poor thing couldn't even form a sentence.

Which was to be expected.

It probably wasn't premeditated, her stealing. Hell, she'd probably never ripped off so much as a packet of sugar from a coffee shop, much less something worth hundreds of dollars from Saks Fifth Avenue, the very definition of American luxury shopping.

But here she was today, motivated by something so strong she'd decided to risk it all—her self respect, her pride, and her clean rap sheet.

I couldn't have found a better mark. I mean, people shoplifted expensive trinkets from upscale stores like Saks all the time, but not many of them would be as stunned as this one was at being caught. Thieves knew they'd be nabbed eventually, right? Or if they didn't, they should.

And if that were the case, then why was the beauty before me so dumbfounded? Did she think it was easy to walk into a store and steal? If it were, everyone would be doing it. Places like Saks would cease to exist.

Seriously. I had half a mind to ask her.

But that was beside the point.

Not ten minutes earlier, I'd been at the men's

tailor on Saks' fourth floor, a little slice of heaven for shoppers like myself who spend as much on bespoke suits as some people make in an entire year. Yeah, that's a douche thing to say, but I work hard for my money, and make no apologies for my spending. I used to go to an old guy down in Little Italy for my clothes, but when I learned my business partners frequented Saks, I decided to patronize the venerable institution, too.

Besides, why go all the way to Lower Manhattan when I could walk a few blocks to one of the most elegant stores in the world and get the same if not better-quality clothing, all delivered with a smile and a blowjob?

I'm not kidding about the blowjob part. Or the smile.

The seamstress I typically got—in my private dressing room, where they would bring you lunch and pretty much anything else you wanted—occasionally offered me a blowie. And I occasionally accepted.

It was just the kind of guy I was.

"Janie," the head tailor had bellowed when I'd arrived, "please take care of Mr. Borroni. I have to step out."

We all knew what that meant.

He shrugged. "I know it's a dirty habit, Leo, but I need my midmorning smoke. If I don't get it, I may just kill someone. And I'd hate to get blood all over these lovely suits." Laughing, he rolled down his shirtsleeves without buttoning the cuffs, pulled on his suit jacket, and hustled for the door.

"Be right back," he called over his shoulder.

And there we were, Janie and I, alone.

She directed me to stand on a little box in front of a three-sided mirror so I could watch her turn my trouser hem from all angles.

"You look real nice today, Mr. Borroni," she said, measuring and pinning the Italian worsted-wool trousers my personal shopper had chosen.

"Thank you, Janie." As I watched her work below, I was distracted by the dark roots where her hair parted —an intense contrast to the rest of her apparently dyed red hair.

"Mr. Borroni, we'll be alone for a good ten minutes or so."

I never got why New Yorkers—or was it all East Coasters?—repeated your name all the time when talking to you. In the West, or at least Las Vegas, nobody did that.

But I'll tell you, New Yorkers lost their shit when I told them I was a Vegas native.

"You're from *Vegas*? I didn't know anybody was *from* Vegas."

Yeah, yeah. Dumb fucks. But I kept it to myself.

Even when they asked silly questions about the desert, like *are the streets covered in sand?* and *are there rattlesnakes everywhere?*

"Mr. Borroni?" Janie ran her fingers up the inside of my thigh, her usual invitation to some adult fun.

Who was I to turn down getting my dick sucked? But just as she reached for the fly on my pants, I took her hand in mine. I just wasn't feeling it.

"Not today, sweetie. But thanks."

She shrugged, her perky expression wavering. "Okay, Mr. Borroni. You can try on your next pair of trousers if you like."

Just then, her boss bustled back in. That was a fast smoke. Thank god I kept my dick in my pants. But on the other hand, would he have cared? Saks *was* all about service.

He inspected her work as she got going on my next pair. "Good job, Janie. Very good job."

I wondered if she blew my business partners, too. I'd have to ask the guys when I saw them later that evening.

Janie might have been a good candidate for our game. But the guys would never approve her. She was too jaded. A little world-weary. And that meant predictable. And predictable killed the risk that made betting so exciting and worthwhile.

No, people who loved gambling the way my boys and I did threw wagers on *un*predictable things. We needed tension. It got our blood running. Our hearts pounding.

No, Janie wasn't a good candidate. Or even a mediocre one.

There were better options. Much better. And one or two were probably cruising around Saks at that very moment.

Janie finished and I got redressed.

"Thank you. Excellent work, as always," I said as I was leaving.

"Our pleasure, Mr. Borroni. We'll have these delivered within the week," she called after me.

But I was already halfway out the door. I was done shopping. It bored me as nothing more than a chore that must be taken care of.

Now, it was time to have fun.

2

LEO

I TOOK the elevator down to Saks' first floor, heading toward the busiest door, which faced Fifth Avenue, where it revolved all day long pulling people in from the street, and spitting them back out onto the crowded sidewalk.

It took me only seconds to find my mark.

She caught my eye with the careful way she'd covet a silk scarf or pair of cashmere gloves, picking them up carefully as if she might be slapped like a little kid for touching something off-limits. She'd study them as if she might buy them, finally flipping over the price tag. If I'd seen it once, I'd seen it a hundred times. A moment of shock—so brief, she might not have realized it—would jolt her when she realized how expensive whatever she was looking at was. She'd return it to where she'd picked it up, like it had never been disturbed.

As if she wasn't allowed to even *think* about owning something so beautiful.

It was like a dance. A graceful, sad dance.

And it was really something to observe.

She was what my mother would have called a *looky-loo.*

One of those people who browsed and browsed and never bought anything.

Not because she couldn't find anything she liked. On the contrary, she loved everything in the store. It's just that, to put it nicely, *nothing was within her budget.*

New York was full of college kids, and I had no doubt this young woman was one of them. The telltale backpack, trendy skinny jeans, down puffer, and white Adidas sneakers were a dead giveaway.

And it wasn't hard to see that she was a broke college student, at that. The girls studying in New York on Daddy's dime floated through stores like Saks as if they were born there. They didn't look at price tags, because prices didn't matter. They just bought the shit they wanted.

But not this one.

At a glance, I figured I knew more about her than she probably did of herself.

Was that arrogant?

Probably.

But there were things a man like me knew.

Her hair was highlighted a buttery blonde, probably to keep up with her fair-haired friends. She got good grades, because she knew that if nothing else, she could always fall back on her education. And she had no idea how beautiful she was, evidenced by her obliviousness to the heads turning in her wake.

I imagined she was from a suburb of New York because she wanted to get away from home, but not go *too far*. It had always been her dream to escape to the *big city*.

Speaking of which, *I* would have been perfectly happy to never have set foot in the place, also known as the shitshow that was Manhattan. But trouble at home had necessitated a break from the desert town where I'd grown up. I'd left Luca, my twin brother and business partner, there and hadn't looked back.

He and I had gone through an ugly gauntlet of shit culminating in the discovery that a longtime family friend and mentor had murdered our mother.

That's right. Our *mother*.

The murdering bastard was one Sal Matteo, head of the Vegas underworld. Also, the man we'd looked up to since we were teenagers, who'd taken us under his wing when our own father had disappeared one day off the face of the earth.

All that changed when Sal, the man we'd loved at least as much as our own dad, had admitted on his deathbed that he'd killed our mother.

I'd never forget it.

He'd kidnapped my brother Luca's girl in a bizarre attempt to claim her for himself. Honestly, he'd never stood a chance. He should have known that. Luca was in love, and you didn't mess with something Luca wanted. Unfortunately, in our efforts to free her, he was shot by one of us—which one, I honestly don't remember. But as he lay in a puddle of blood, and while my brother solemnly and regretfully knelt at his side holding his hand during his final breaths, Sal had made his deathbed confession. Whether it was to ease our conscience or punish my brother and me for eternity, I didn't know.

But I'd never forgive him either way. And now he was six feet under, where he belonged for helping himself to two things not meant for him—both our mother *and* Luca's woman.

Apparently, Sal and my mom had been an item for a time, but strictly on the down low. I'd never had a clue, and neither had my brother. When she'd wanted to go public with their relationship, Sal had silenced her the only way he knew how.

And then he'd confessed it to us after we'd wondered for years who would have gunned her down as she left her weekly hair appointment. Those were dark days, which got even darker after Sal's admission. Luca stayed in Vegas to keep the family businesses moving forward. But I got the fuck out.

Startling me out of my reverie and bringing me back to Saks and my pretty looky-loo, a soft hand landed on the forearm of my expensive suit jacket. "May I help you, sir?" an ethereal sales clerk asked.

"No, thank you. Just browsing."

She tilted her head. "Well then. Please let me know if there's *anything* I can do for you." She stared a moment longer, then floated away. Damn. That was *some* kind of service.

My attention turned back to the college girl and I did a double take as she rounded the corner to a jewelry counter.

She looked like someone from my past. Someone long gone.

Maybe that was that why I was drawn to her.

She was so preoccupied, she didn't notice me standing opposite as she gazed into a jewelry case. The irises of her blue eyes were lighter in the middle with a dark ring around the edges. Her bottom lip, which she seemed to be in the habit of biting, was full and juicy, and her nails were bitten to the quick. And when she walked away, she gave me a perfect view of the curvy upside-down heart that was her ass.

But what really got me was the bold expression she wore. Perhaps that was why none of the store clerks were approaching her. Of course, it might also have been the broke-college-girl air she gave off, too.

In any case, she'd perfected *resting bitch face*, I think it was called.

She'd moved to the handbags, so I followed, discreetly, of course, where a quick glance told me they were in the five-hundred-dollars-and-up range. My mark had good taste. Expensive taste.

If you're going to be a crook, you might as well go big.

She fingered a couple bags, and then a couple more. Selecting one, she inspected it inside and out, running her fingers over the pale pink fabric that covered it.

I could almost hear the conversation she was having with herself: *Is this the one I want? And how badly do I want it?*

After a brief conversation with the same sales clerk who'd approached me, she looked left and right to determine if the coast were clear, then slipped the object of her affection into the shopping bag dangling from her wrist.

Boom. She'd done it.

My lovely little college co-ed was a thief.

Glancing around, her expression morphed from defiance, to fear, and back again.

An evening bag? Strange fare for a broke college student, but you never knew about people.

I scanned the area, too, to see if the saleslady who'd offered me assistance had seen anything. But she was off with another customer, luckily for my thief, who, if she were going to make a habit of shoplifting, had some work to do on her technique.

But that was not my problem.

Getting her out of Saks without being arrested by store security *was*.

She looked around one more time, then hightailed it toward the door. In her sneakers, she could probably run like hell if she had to.

But I was faster. I was always faster.

As my fingers encircled her arm, before she realized what was happening, she tried to jerk out of my grip in unconscious resistance. To emphasize the gravity of the situation, I tightened my hold. That's when I got her attention.

What had driven her to steal? Some sort of desperation brought on by shame or just a plain old compulsion to have something that, in her mind, everyone around her already had?

Why not me? was a manner of thinking that justified all sorts of behavior, thievery included. Fascinating how much you could learn by watching someone for a few minutes.

And exciting as hell. I was a sick fuck, I'd be the first to admit it. Her vulnerable demeanor, with a slight but transparent overlay of *I'm a tough girl*, got me twitching in the dick department. I loved nothing more than a woman who tried to be a badass and just couldn't pull it off no matter how hard she tried. And now that I was close to her, I could smell the scent of plain, clean girl and some sort of cheap drugstore shampoo—not to mention, fear—something else that got my motor revving. My business partners could take the overly perfumed, tarted-up dolls that usually came our way. No, thanks.

I'd found what I was looking for—it was sweet, innocent, clean, and *mine*.

3

MARAY

"Damn. Your boobs look so good in that top."

Loud sigh. "Really? I don't know. I still want a boob job. I need it. I mean, look at these tiny tits. My mom promised if I got straight A's."

Tongue clucking. "Jesus. Your mom drives a hard bargain."

"Yeah. She's such a bitch."

More sighs.

As I towel-dried my hair in the room I shared with Vivian, Lulu's and Aimee's gripes about the unfairness of the world drifted my way from their room next door. Even if I'd not recognized their shrill and entitled voices, I knew they were pretty much the only girls around who'd call their mothers bitches for making them work for a boob job.

We didn't live in a sorority house, per se. Since we were on an urban campus in New York City, our sorority had rented the better part of an apartment building. We had three floors and a large communal bathroom per floor. We kept our bedroom doors open most of the time since it took key cards to access the building and elevator. The place was like a fortress, which was fine with me, and created an insular pod of rich-girl heaven.

The only problem was that I wasn't a rich girl.

Thanks to tight security, the worst crime to take place in our secluded little world was usually nothing more than someone borrowing your clothes—without asking. Which happened a lot. And was the cause of many fights.

Although, no one borrowed my clothes. Not usually, anyway. Mine weren't 'borrowable,' if you wanted to know the truth.

I was more than a little different from most of the girls I lived with.

"Hey, what're you wearing to the formal?" I overheard Lulu ask Aimee.

I pulled on my jeans and Bagelry T-shirt, the uniform I wore to my crappy part-time bagel shop job, and continued eavesdropping.

"I guess I'll wear my blue dress," Aimee said, most likely shrugging as if she'd just made the hardest decision she ever would.

"Why not wear the black one? You know, with the

open back. That dress is so hot with your blonde hair," Lulu said.

"You're right. I do look good in that dress. But I promised to let Maray borrow it."

My ears perked up at the sound of my name. There was silence for a moment, and I could picture Lulu rolling her eyes. "You're letting *her* borrow it? Does she ever *not* need to borrow something from one of us?"

"Well, I don't mind. I mean, she is a sponge, but she's nice, and I feel kind of bad for her."

She felt *bad*? For *me*?

And I was a *sponge*?

They went on chattering, but I didn't hear any of it. Blood rushed through my ears, and I sat on my bed for a moment to make sure I didn't puke.

So *that's* how it was.

And that was the moment when my life started going sideways.

I knew I wasn't exactly from their world. Okay, I wasn't from their world, at all.

I didn't live off my parents' credit cards, and I didn't look forward to inheriting a trust fund when I turned twenty-five or whatever. But I also didn't know these girls' generosity and willingness to loan me dresses for our fancy formals and other parties came with so much resentment.

Was I that oblivious to their apparent superiority?

Jesus, was I naïve.

Those girls were my sorority sisters. But I guess that didn't mean they were my friends.

I silently pulled on my Converse Chucks and grabbed my jacket and backpack. Slipping out of my room, I headed in the direction where I wouldn't have to pass their open door. It meant I had to walk down several flights of stairs instead of taking the elevator, but at least they wouldn't know I'd heard them and I wouldn't have to see their bitchy faces.

What other shit were they saying about me? Actually, I didn't need to know. Didn't want to, either. I'd heard all I needed to, or could swallow, at the moment.

I headed into the brisk fall breeze blowing down the street toward the one class I had before work.

It was a class I enjoyed, a lot—Statistics, if you could believe it—especially since the instructor was a hunk. But at that moment in time, the usual spring in my step was absent, thanks to the gossipy bitches I'd just overheard. In fact, I felt like I'd been run over by a truck. Each step forward took a huge amount of effort, and the growing lump in my throat was getting the better of me.

Why did I care what those girls thought of me? I knew I shouldn't. My down-to-earth, public school-teacher parents would never approve of them. But, truth was, I saw girls like that as a sort of metaphorical gauntlet I needed to pass through to achieve the life I wanted. If I could navigate them, I could navigate anywhere and anything.

Including getting myself an expensive education at a private university that really should have been beyond reach for someone like me.

To hell with those bitches. I wouldn't go to the damn formal. That would show them.

Unfortunately, that wasn't a realistic option. For better or for worse, I was the organizer of the event, something I'd cheerfully signed up for at the beginning of the semester. I wanted to prove my leadership skills and show these privileged girls that I could put on an event that would put theirs to shame.

And now, here I was, the one walking around with my head hanging down.

Maybe I could use studying as an excuse to bail on the formal? I could say I had a kick-ass exam staring me down. Or, that I needed to go home for the weekend to see my parents for something unexpected.

Fuck me.

I settled into my chair in the half-full school auditorium and pulled out my notebook. The instructor dove into his lesson but instead of listening to information I usually devoured, I found myself doodling, unable to concentrate.

So I got up and left.

4

MARAY

I HAD some time to kill before my shift at Bagelry, so I moseyed along, dreamily eyeing the shop windows of Lower Manhattan. When people said New York was a shopper's paradise, they weren't kidding. There was something for everyone here.

Except for me.

I could always try to buy a dress for the damn formal. That way I could take the one Aimee was lending me and throw it back in her nose-jobbed face. But honestly, my minimum-wage job at Bagelry didn't allow for such luxuries.

No, I would wear the damn dress and hold my head up.

As if I had any other choice.

But I still needed shoes and a bag. Vivian would

loan me her strappy silver heels. But that was it. I wasn't borrowing anything else. I'd find a way to get my own evening bag.

I hustled over to the Goodwill store two blocks down, fingers crossed I might come across some sort of treasure that a luckier girl had decided she no longer needed. But as I dug through the racks there, I realized the only thing I could possibly walk out with would scream *second hand* louder than I was willing to risk.

Plan foiled.

Then I had a second idea.

I ran back to my building and headed to my room, speeding past the bitches.

"Maray. Hey," one of them called.

People loved to say rhyme things with my name. *Say, Maray* was a big one, too.

"Oh, hi, guys. Didn't know you were around," I lied.

I looked from one to the other. Their faces gave away nothing. If I hadn't heard them, I'd still think they were my friends. I'd never have suspected they'd called me a *sponge.* It might have been a small insult, but it stung like a bitch. And I wouldn't forget it anytime soon, if ever.

"Coming home from class?" Lulu asked, surveying her eyelash extensions in a handheld mirror.

I nodded as I kept walking. "Yup. On my way to work."

"At Bagelry? You're so *lucky* you get to work there.

Hey, will you bring us home the day-olds? They're so good," Aimee said.

My sorority sisters had fallen into the habit of expecting leftover bagels every time I worked, since I often covered closing shift. But to say I was *lucky* I worked there?

Now I was reading meaning into everything they said.

"'Course. You know I always hook you up," I said, ducking into my room.

I went straight for my roommate Vivian's closet. She was a world-class spender, and I knew she'd have an empty shopping bag or two from some fancy store. I pulled the books out of my backpack and tossed them on my bed, stuffing a crisply folded Saks Fifth Avenue shopping bag in their place. It would have killed Viv to fold even a pair of her underwear, but her souvenirs of expensive shopping trips were treasured and treated with reverence, like the bag. I ran for the elevator.

"Don't forget my bagels!" Lulu hollered after me.

"I won't," I answered as the elevator doors closed.

I grabbed the subway to head uptown to Saks. I knew they had great stuff, not because I'd ever shopped there, but because most of the girls in my sorority did. If I got up there in ten minutes, looked around, and gave myself ten minutes to get back, I'd only be a few minutes late for work. There'd be *something* there I could afford, right, if I took on some extra shifts at the bagel shop?

Mel, the cranky, imperious owner, would undoubtedly scold me, but I really didn't give a shit at that point. I hated him and his shop, but needed to have some sort of job as part of my work-study agreement.

I got off the subway at Forty-Ninth Street and Fifth Avenue, wondering how much an evening bag might be. Maybe fifty bucks? I had a little over a hundred in my checking account, so I could splurge if I really had to.

Standing outside the store, I took a deep breath as if I were entering someplace sacred and holy, which in a sense, I guess I was. Some people had church, and some people had Saks. The revolving doors, which terrified me with their relentless spinning, deposited me inside the hallowed shopping mecca, which I took in like I'd discovered heaven.

The perfect lighting and perfumed air assaulted my senses with their bold glamour, stopping me as soon as I'd gotten through the possessed door—which was not smart because everyone behind me had to squeeze by. But as soon as the initial shock of being surrounded by expensive perfection subsided, I stepped out of the way and scrolled through my phone, pretending to be looking for something important. What I was really doing was trying to figure out where the handbags were without asking one of the model-perfect clerks floating around, smiling and helping people spend money on expensive, beautiful things.

Did clerks like that help people like me?

I wasn't so sure.

So I did the only thing I could think of, which was to look up the online store directory.

Bingo.

Bags were on the opposite side of the floor where I'd entered.

I wove through the maze of mini-shops that included jewelry, perfume, makeup, and stockings, pausing to look, admire, and touch as if I might make a purchase.

Then I found the handbags.

Holy crap.

If I hadn't already been self-conscious of my ratty backpack, I now wanted to crawl under one of the store's display tables.

The designer names blew me away: Chloé, Fendi, Chanel, and more. I was clearly in the wrong place.

But then I spotted a table marked *Sale.*

Yes.

I sauntered over to find there was nothing under five hundred dollars.

On sale.

Five hundred dollars. And up.

Well, shit.

But, to look like one of the cool kids, I pulled the Saks shopping bag out of my backpack and hung it on my wrist.

I wasn't an idiot. I knew a few things about pretending to belong.

And my new accessory, even though it swung empty, did give me a boost of confidence. I held my head higher while perusing the merchandise.

That's right. I was *perusing*.

I examined bag after bag, as if I might really purchase one. I ran my fingers across soft leather, pebbled leather, and suede leather, opening and closing their latches and looking into their pockets. These works of art not only felt expensive, they also *smelled* expensive and *sounded* expensive, their metal clasps snapping *just so*.

Then I found the evening bags, and my god, they were miniature jewels of perfection, each more beautiful than the one before it, available in every color of the rainbow. But the ones that caught my eye were the bags encrusted with jewels. Holy crap.

The *Judith Leibers*. Yup. Even *I* knew of her fabled whimsical evening bags shaped like cupcakes, gumball machines, ladybugs, and anything else a rich lady might desire. Generally appealing to the 'older' crowd, these babies were as iconic as their designer.

And then I saw *my* holy grail of evening bags. Like a moth to flame, I was drawn to a smooth oval shaped number in pale pink silk, with a small chain from which to dangle it.

I dared pick it up and found it fit perfectly into my hand. And it would go perfectly with the dress I was to borrow from Aimee for the formal. The dress I'd rather *not* borrow, but which I had no choice about.

That Maray. She's such a sponge.

I blinked away the tears burning my eyes. I had to remain focused and calm. I was holding a treasure in my hand. A treasure the likes of which I may never hold again.

"May I help you, miss?"

A polite and smiling clerk startled the shit out of me. In fact, she startled me so badly I nearly dropped the bag. But I recovered.

I was nothing if not resilient.

"Oh, thank you. It's so beautiful," I gushed. As if I might really buy it.

"May I show you something?" she asked, reaching for it.

With her hair pulled back into a tight bun and her glossy lipstick, I didn't think I'd ever seen a more perfect human.

"Sure," I said, handing it to her reluctantly. I'd wanted to hold it for just a little longer but what could I do?

She must have seen my face fall and handed it back to me. "Oh. Here. Let's have you do it."

She pointed at the clasp. "With just a little twist right there, you can open a secret compartment."

Was she serious? Good lord. I really had stumbled across a treasure.

"A secret compartment?" I croaked, as the little bag opened like a flower, with more compartments than I could ever hope to fill.

Okay, now my eyes were really tearing up. Shit.

The compartments provided plenty of room for a lipstick, keys, a credit card, a little cash, and maybe a condom. Or two.

It was perfection, wrapped in silk.

"Um," I stumbled, "how much is it?"

The clerk smiled politely again because, of course, and pulled a small price tag out of one of the bag's hidden pockets. She flipped it over and announced the price like she was saying it might rain that day.

"Eight hundred seventy-five." She tucked the tag back in. "I'll let you look it over while you decide." She patted my arm and walked away, like I might actually buy it.

Shit. Why couldn't this woman be one of my sorority sisters? I wanted to kiss her for not shaming me for looking like a poor schlub who could never afford an evening bag that cost as much as my rent.

She floated over to another customer, probably someone who could actually spend some money in the store. I didn't blame her.

I started putting the bag back on the display, but it somehow wouldn't leave my fingers—or maybe it was my fingers that wouldn't leave *it*. I held it in my hand, continuing to rub my thumb over the silk.

Then, without giving it much thought, I dropped it into my Saks shopping bag and headed for the door.

I told myself it was just one time. One time in my twenty years of life that I would be a criminal. One time that I would take something that didn't belong to me. That's it.

Only one time.

Maybe I'd even bring the purse back when I was done with it.

Actually, who was I kidding? The thing was fucking perfection. I was going to keep it until the day I died.

And in the few seconds between placing it in my shopping bag and reaching the door, while I fantasized about how it would improve my life on so many levels, a hand closed around my arm.

A male hand, both very big and very strong.

5

MARAY

MY GAZE FOLLOWED the hand that had closed around my upper arm, to the face of probably the most gorgeous man I'd ever seen.

Thick, black, combed-back hair, a perfectly chiseled chin and strong brow, and enough facial scruff to be sexy and stylish without being sloppy completed the picture.

But his dark eyes were cold, offering nothing, and he wore the slightest smirk. I scanned him and in a flash wondered when store security had gotten so well dressed and so perfectly good-looking. Maybe I should consider stealing more often.

Kidding.

In about sixty seconds, I'd pretty much ruined my life.

Yup, it was over. I'd thought I had problems before?

That shit had been child's play.

The pettiness of the sorority, the small humiliations of working for Mel, and the struggles to stay awake through boring lectures. I'd thought that was hard?

Well, look at me now.

"Come with me, miss," the man growled.

Security men *growled*? Guess Saks hired extra-mean ones.

I looked around, and the nice sales clerk who'd shown me the secret compartment? Her back was to us as she helped someone who probably wasn't stealing.

And what was perhaps most disturbing about the whole thing was that I was more concerned that she should see me in my moment of shame than anyone else.

The shopping bag containing the contraband was whipped out of my hand, and before I even realized what was happening, handcuffs clicked and tightened on my wrists.

They were cold and they were uncomfortable, which I guess was the point.

The man I was with threw a jacket or something over my hands to hide the cuffs, just like they did in the movies. And just like they did in the movies, I held my head in shame while I was escorted out the door, into the chilly New York evening.

It hadn't yet occurred to me yet to ask why we were

leaving the store. At that point, I was preoccupied with making my shift at Bagelry. As if.

"Um, sir, could we talk about this for a second?" I asked, swallowing as much indignity as I could.

He navigated us onto the sidewalk where New Yorkers, possibly the fastest-walking people on earth, poured around us as if we were a rock impeding, but not stopping, the flow of a stream.

"What is it you'd like to discuss, miss?" he asked gruffly.

Cripes, the way this man stared at me. One on hand, the little shiver running up my spine told me to be scared, but on the other, I had this odd sensation that he felt for me. Which made no sense since his eyes were nothing but pools of brown so dark they were nearly black.

What did I want to discuss? Hmmm. Good question. I had nothing, actually, and as the reality of the situation washed over me, I began to shiver, even though my brow was damp and a trickle of perspiration ran between my boobs.

Why had I needed so badly to impress a couple sorority girls, anyway? It wasn't like I was going to fool them into believing I suddenly had enough money to shop at Saks. It wasn't like the guy I was crushing on, Thomas, who'd be at the formal, was suddenly going to start paying attention to me.

Hey, look at Maray. She's got an expensive evening bag!
Yeah, no.

MIKA LANE

The only time that douchebag showed me any attention was when a party was winding down, everyone was drunk, and there were pretty much no other girls left for him to hit on.

So, yeah, I'd sucked face with him. I might have even let him touch my boob.

But only one.

What *the fuck* had I been thinking?

Just like I could have made a different choice, I also could have chosen a different life path, like one where I went to the closest state university to home and commuted from my parents' house. It would have kind of sucked, but I would have been with *my* people. People who'd come from nice, middle-class families. Not kids who hated their parents but spent their money anyway, who went skiing for Christmas, to the Caribbean for spring break, and to Europe for the summer.

I'd never done any of those things. It wasn't looking like I ever would.

I could see it. What the fuck was I, a finance major —*a finance major!*—doing stealing? I was supposed to be the epitome of responsibility. I was the one from my high school who was going to Make It Big.

I'd just shot that all right to hell.

I looked at the security man who'd just busted me, in his nice suit and perfectly knotted tie, wishing he'd been one of the dumpy security guys you saw in the movies. Christ, I was thinking about how hot he was when I should have been focused on survival.

Could I deny taking the purse?

I had no proof I'd bought it—no receipt, and no pretty tissue paper wrapping that things legitimately purchased at Saks got.

I wasn't much of a liar, anyway.

"I wonder if you could just let me put the purse back and forget it ever happened," I suggested cheerfully.

No harm in asking.

But he stared at me like I was an idiot.

I tried another approach. "If that doesn't work for you, could we go back inside and I'll just pay for the bag?" I offered.

I *might* have enough room on my credit card to pay for it. That would buy some time, and maybe I could give him the slip.

No go. "Miss, you need to come with me to head-quarters."

What the hell were *headquarters*?

"I'm afraid I can't, sir. I have my shift at Bagelry. In fact, I'm already late. I have to close tonight."

Nice try.

He shook his head regretfully, but he probably wasn't half as disappointed as my sorority sisters would be when they found they were being cheated out of their day-old bagels.

"We're going down to the station," he said.

I was no expert in shoplifting, but I remembered when a kid from high school had gotten caught, that the police had come to the store. Not the other way around.

"Um, that doesn't sound like normal protocol to me."

He tilted his head, and while annoyance passed over his face, he also, strangely, looked like he was enjoying himself. Probably one of those alpha-hole power-hungry security dudes who lived to shake people up.

"This way, miss," he said, guiding me toward a black car.

I hesitated as he directed me toward the vehicle. "Um, where did you say we were going?"

"The station." He pulled open the back door.

A man popped out of the driver's seat and made his way over to me.

Guess they'd been through this before, because the man uncuffed me with a grim smile, slid my pack down my shoulders, and helped me in. The security guy threw my shopping bag and backpack in the front seat and crawled in back with me.

I'd never seen arrests play out like this in the movies, but then when was my life ever like a movie?

6

LEO

So far so good.

As soon as my lovely mark was in the car, Smitt maneuvered into heavy Manhattan traffic. I'd gotten her out of Saks before the real store security, or cameras, noticed her. Pulling a notepad out of my breast pocket, I made like I was going to take notes.

"Your name, miss?"

"Maray. Maray Stone," she answered dutifully.

I'd taken a risk removing her cuffs, and now she was looking around the car for an escape route. I braced myself for some swinging.

"Is everything okay, Miss Stone?" I asked.

She nervously wiped her palms on the legs of her jeans and narrowed her eyes at me. "Are you a police officer? Or store security? Where are we going?"

Ah, she was catching on. Smart girl. Not just pretty, but smart.

"I'm actually neither," I said, leaning back to take her in.

Her brow furrowed, as I'd hope it would. After all, playing with an idiot would have been no fun.

She craned her neck toward Smitt in the front seat, addressing him. "Is this some kind of joke?"

He said nothing.

I watched her hand creep toward the door handle. Couldn't blame her. I would have tried to get out, too.

But the handle didn't budge. I steeled myself for her realization that things were not as they seemed.

"What the fuck? Why won't the door handle open? This is bullshit." She pounded on the window.

But Smitt just drove faster.

My years working the criminal underworld had given me excellent reflexes, and Maray didn't stand a chance when she balled up her fist and tried to slug me.

Poor thing. She was getting upset.

I caught her by the wrists before she was in striking distance to my—well, I wasn't sure where she'd wanted to punch me, because her arms were honestly just flailing.

"Maray, calm down or I'll put the cuffs back on. Do you want that?" I asked her gently, holding her still.

She leaned toward me, seething frustration. "I don't give a shit about your cuffs. Let me out of here. You're not a cop, are you? Neither of you are," she argued, gesturing toward Smitt with her chin.

I held her while she tried to twist away. Of course, she didn't stand a chance. But I was glad she was at least trying. And god, was she beautiful when she was pissed.

"You've committed a crime, Maray. You have to pay the price."

My reminder quieted her, and she took a long, deep breath. "Fine. But who the hell are you to merit punishment? You're not a cop *or* store security. Are you *kidnapping* me?" she asked indignantly.

I shook my head slowly, my gaze locked with hers. Christ, she was gorgeous, all blonde hair flying around her face as she had her shit fit.

"I wouldn't think of this as kidnapping. It's more of a rescue, if you want to know the truth," I said.

She glowered at me, and I felt a second twinge beneath the belt. God, I loved a feisty woman. She knew she'd made a mistake—and a big one at that—but she still had enough self-respect to stick up for herself.

"What the hell does that mean, a *rescue*?" she spat.

"Do you know what would have happened, had you been taken by store security?"

She paused for a moment. "I would have been arrested. You know, whatever they do with shoplifters."

I nodded slowly, waiting for her to continue. But she didn't, which told me she had no idea of what she was up against.

"You would have been arrested, that's correct. But that's just the beginning."

With her arms crossed defiantly, she frowned. "What does that mean?"

"Hold on," I said, reaching for the phone in my breast pocket.

I swiped to open a call from my brother in Vegas. My little prisoner could wait.

The noise in the background was raucous. "Hey, bro. What's up?" he said. "I'm waiting for Echo so we can go to dinner."

After our former mentor, Sal, had admitted he'd murdered our mother, Luca had needed to scale back on the family business for sanity's sake. Opening a down-to-earth diner specializing in homemade pies with his new love, Echo, had seemed like just the ticket. I'd thought it was a ridiculous idea. Neither of us knew the restaurant business, but in no time the place was the talk of the town and making a killing—not an easy feat in the foodie town that Vegas had in recent years turned into.

And the name of the new diner was Dirty Game, inspired by a something my brother and I used to play. But that was all behind us now.

I'd moved on to other kinks.

"Hey, Luc. Bringing a new friend to the club. Seeing if she's up for the Bet." I winked at Maray, whose arms were still crossed. And man, could she throw a good stink eye.

"Leo, are you still playing that shit?" he asked.

Yeah, he was the older, responsible one. If being older by five minutes counted.

"Dude, you know I like playing the ponies. So to speak," I said.

It was easy for Luca to be critical. Shit always worked out for him. I mean, no one had the perfect life, but he'd always seemed to get by with less effort than most.

Not so much the case with me.

He didn't sound happy, but that was too bad. "I know you like playing with fire, bro, but be careful," he said.

Smitt turned the corner toward the club, and Maray was getting more steamed by the minute. It was time to wrap things up.

"Gotta go, man, but before I do, how's Echo?" I asked.

True happiness poured out of his voice. "Oh, she's great. Getting bigger by the day."

Yeah, his woman was *with child*. Another way that life just worked out for him. I was happy for them, though, and tried to push from my mind the shit hand I'd been dealt in that area.

"Awesome. Gotta go. Call ya later." I swiped my phone closed. I wasn't in the mood for the morality police. I'd never played by the rules before. Wasn't about to start now.

7

LEO

ONCE IN THE PARKING GARAGE, I extended my hand to Maray to help her exit the car.

But she scooted across the seat, away from me, pressing herself against the opposite side of the car. The movement opened her jacket and stretched her T-shirt over her chest, showcasing some lovely round breasts.

I leaned into the car. "Please come with me, Maray."

"What is this place?" she asked, looking out the car window in a panic.

Unfortunately for her, Smitt got out of the driver's seat and opened the door on the side of the car where she was leaning. Before she realized she'd been tag-teamed, Smitt had her on her feet.

"Hey!" she yelled.

"We can put the handcuffs back on, if you prefer," I said, taking hold of one of her arms as Smitt and I led her to the parking garage elevator.

She struggled, but mostly for effect. By now, she undoubtedly knew she wouldn't get away. "No, please, no more handcuffs," she said.

I pressed the *close* button once inside the elevator. "You've been brought to my club."

Her squirming subsided, but I held my grip. This provided an excuse to stand closer, and I found myself dying to brush the loose blonde hairs off her face.

She frowned. "A club? What kind of club? On my god. You're a sex trafficker, aren't you?" Her face began to crumble, and she hung her head. "I'll never see my parents again," she whispered.

"Maray. Maray, look at me." I hooked a finger under her chin. "This is not about sex trafficking. Put that out of your mind right now."

Sniffling, she held her head up bravely. "Then, what is it?"

"Have a look for yourself," I said. The elevator doors opened to a room with three round poker tables.

At one table, the only game on at the moment, were four gentlemen and one of our dealers. Hovering nearby was our server tasked with keeping the players' drinks full.

"What are they playing?" Maray asked as I hurried her past the game.

My players valued their privacy.

"High-stakes poker."

She stopped again and turned to me. "Card games? You play card games here? Why all the secrecy? And security?" she asked, gesturing at the guards flanking the elevators.

"Do you know what high stakes means?" Of course she didn't. "Our players are famous people—politicians, athletes, financiers, actors—who are very, very wealthy. They expect the utmost discretion. And they are also betting large sums of money. More than many people make in a year. Or a lifetime, depending on the game. *That's* why we have security."

We entered a small room with a table and two chairs, where on occasion we interviewed prospective players. It was vital to do some profiling to make sure we admitted the right kind of players—those who could truly afford our high-dollar bets, and who could afford to occasionally lose a shit ton of money if they weren't doing well on a given night. We didn't want people gambling away the family farm, so to speak.

There was also a large one-way mirror on the wall where the interviewee could be watched from the outside.

"Have a seat," I offered, snagging the chair with its back to the mirror. The only remaining seat faced out.

"You haven't told me your name." She folded her hands neatly on the table, like she was in a job interview.

Fair enough.

"I am Leo Borroni. I own this card club with several business partners."

She looked at me like she was rolling my name over in her mind. As if she might have heard of me, which was unlikely. I kept a very low profile.

"How long have you being doing, um, this?" she asked, waving her hand around.

She was gathering information. I liked that. And now that I was seated opposite her and could fully appreciate her entirety, I couldn't take my eyes off her. Sure, she was dressed like a broke college student, but I didn't care about shit like that. And yeah, she was naturally beautiful with her piercing blue eyes and full lips. But what went a long way with me was how proud she was.

"May I call you Leo?" she asked.

Here come the negotiations.

I sat back in my chair and loosened my tie. "Of course."

Looking at her hands, she took a deep breath. "Leo, I think we can work this thing out here."

Something in the way she said that really got me going. Nodding for her to continue, I shifted in my trousers to make room for my growing cock.

"This can all be resolved, can't it? Let me go. I'll take the purse back. Or—I tell you what—you keep it. Give it to your girlfriend or your mother."

I almost felt a little guilty about having so much fun. Almost.

When I didn't respond, her voice inched a tad higher. "I have a full ride to a private university. I come from a nice family. I'm a finance major," she pleaded.

I was going to let her go on for a while before I started *my* line of questioning.

She searched my face for some sort of understanding. Or maybe it was compassion.

"I... I'm a nice girl, Leo."

"That's one thing we agree on," I said, surprising her after being silent.

"Um, what?"

Her hands were no longer folded neatly on the table but were now balled into fists, her knuckles turning white.

"I know you're a nice girl. That's why I'm wondering why you stole the purse."

Defiance crossed her face again. "I'm wondering why you care," she said, thrusting her chin at me.

"Just curious, is all."

She looked around wildly. "*Just curious*? Are you kidding? Tell me what the hell am I doing here."

"You'll know soon, Maray. You'll know soon."

8

LEO

I EXITED THE INTERVIEW ROOM, pulling the door closed behind me, leaving Maray alone to think about her situation. As expected, two of my business partners were watching through the one-way glass.

"Hey, guys. What do you think?" I asked.

Colt put his hands on his hips and nodded. "She's gorgeous. I'm down with that girl-next-door look. It's refreshing after the usual skanks we get in here."

I rolled my eyes. "Thanks, Colt. That's really helpful."

I turned to Dom. "So? What do you think?"

He raised his massive shoulders and cracked his neck, like he always did when he was thinking. "I think she'll play. I mean, she's kind of resistant right now, but she'll fall in line. You said she tried to steal something?"

Locked in the interview room, Maray was looking around as if she might find an escape.

Good luck with that. Even if she did find a way out of the room, security would stop her before she made it halfway to the elevator.

"She stole a purse from Saks. I think the dollar amount was over eight hundred."

Colt exhaled with a low whisper. "Felony."

"Yup. And she probably had no idea," Dom added.

Nico came flying out of his office, tucking in his shirt and straightening his tie.

Jesus, that guy.

"Dude, were you just doing someone in your office?" I asked.

He avoided my gaze and looked through the glass at Maray. "Mind ya business, brother."

I'd asked him time and again to get his pussy elsewhere. Fucking women at work was not good for business. But did he listen to me?

Hell no.

"She's a looker, for sure. Very sweet," he said, gesturing at the window. "What did she do?"

"Shoplifted a big-ticket item," Dom answered.

Nico smirked. "Bad choice, little girl," he growled. "Do you think she'd be game for a little group activity?" He looked from one to the other of us with his evil smile.

Colt laughed. "Oh yeah, what do they call that now,

when a woman has all the dudes instead of the other way around? A reverse harem or something?"

Dom nodded. "Yeah, dude. I've heard it called that. Great name," he said, rolling his eyes.

"Reverse harem? What the fuck is that?" Nico asked.

I raised my hands in the *stop* position. "Guys. Can we focus here? We have some important decisions to make."

"Dude, I just wanna see her naked—" Nico said.

"I know. I know. You want to see every female naked because you can only think with your little head. But what we need to do right now is decide if we are taking bets on her or not. Will she join in the program?"

There was a ruckus in the game room behind us. I peeked around the corner, and all was well. One of our louder patrons had apparently won a big hand. He was jumping up and down while the other players rolled their eyes at him. So much for 'poker face.'

Before anyone could respond, our beautiful server and all-round everything girl, Samia, approached us with four whiskeys on her tray.

"Gentlemen," she said, offering the beverages with her perfect Mona Lisa smile.

"Yes. Just what the doctor ordered. Thank you, Samia," Nico said, downing his whiskey in one gulp, then turning to watch her walk away.

Had he fucked her, too?

"What do you know about her, Leo?" Colt asked.

Not much. But enough.

"College girl on scholarship. Finance major—"

Nico snorted. "Guess they forgot to teach her shoplifting an item over five hundred dollars is a felony in New York state."

Dom chuckled.

I continued. "Seems like she's from a pretty straight middle-class family."

"Why'd she steal?" Colt asked.

I shook my head. "I didn't get that far with her."

Colt shook his head, followed by Dom. "Until we know her motive, we can't really bet on how far she'll go."

These guys made me tired.

"That's the point of the bets. We don't *have* complete information. We make our decisions based on what we know," I insisted.

"All right. All right," Colt said, holding his hands up in surrender. "I think she's gonna shut you down, flat. I'm betting against her all the way."

I looked at Nico and Dom. "What about you guys?"

Nico stared through the window. "What do *you* think, Leo?"

"I think she'll be on board."

He nodded. "I do, too. She doesn't want to fuck up her ride."

"That leaves you, Dom."

He cracked his neck again. "I think she'll start, but

not finish. That's what I'm betting on. She won't have the stomach for the program."

Any one of us could have been right about her. That's what made our game so much fun.

"Okay then. Let's see what she says," I said, heading back to the interview room.

"Make us proud, brother," Nico called after me.

9

LEO

I EYED the Diet Coke can in Maray's hand. "I see Samia brought you something to drink. Would you like anything else? Maybe something to eat?" I took the seat opposite her.

Her hair fell into her face as she shook her head, glaring at me.

I was dying to kiss her. I mean, she was clearly vulnerable but trying so hard to be badass. Hot. And I could just imagine her under me, maybe a little shy at first, but then opening up like a blooming flower...

Down, boy.

I took a deep breath and leaned into the table between us. "My business partners and I have a proposition for you."

Time to negotiate. My pulse was picking up. This

part was almost more fun than waiting for the outcome.

"You have a choice to make, Maray," I continued.

She pursed her lips. "A choice? Are you kidding me? I'm a fucking prisoner. Prisoners don't have choices."

Damn. The f-bomb. Now my dick was really getting hard.

"You'll be free to go soon. Just listen to what I have to say."

Her eyes widened. "You're letting me go?"

I laughed. "Of course. You can't stay here forever. So, here's the deal. We can either turn you in to Saks for shoplifting, or you can do some tasks as designated by my business partners and me. We will be making wagers on how or whether you are able to complete them."

She frowned, as I expected her to. It really wasn't much of a choice, when you came down to it. But that's what happens when you're a thief.

Yeah, she was a thief.

"Okayyyy… so what are these tasks? They better not be anything sexual." She crossed her arms in a defensive move.

I shook my head. "No, they are not sexual. You don't have to worry about that."

"All right. What are they?"

I sat back in my chair. It was hard to describe The Bet.

"You will commit a series of petty crimes. Stealing newspapers. Things like that."

She rolled her eyes. "The price I have to pay for shoplifting an evening bag is to steal more stuff? That's ridiculous," she huffed.

I shrugged. "Maybe it is. But that's our offer. You can complete the program or be arrested. Your choice."

She stood, pulling on her jacket. "Take me back to Saks. I'll pay the price for what I did there and be done with you and your crazy business partners." She used air quotes around 'business partners.'

She paced around the small room, giving the guys on the other side of the one-way mirror an eyeful of her curvy ass.

I knew I'd hear about that later from Nico. He was probably already planning ways to get her pants off, the horny bastard.

"There's one thing you need to know first, Maray."

"Yeah?" she asked, whirling around to look at me.

I had to hand it to her. She was feisty. But I was about to drop my bomb.

"The purse you stole has a retail value of over eight hundred dollars."

She rolled her eyes. "No kidding. You think I don't know that?"

"What I'm pretty sure you *don't* know," I said in my most patient voice, "is that anything shoplifted, valued at over five hundred dollars, is a felony in New York."

"Um. What?" she stumbled.

63

Of course she didn't know that. How the hell would she? It wasn't like she was a career criminal.

"The value of the merchandise you stole puts your theft in the felony category. I assume you have no priors, but it could still mean a short stint in prison. You could lose your free ride at school and have a very hard time finding future employment."

My information had the desired effect. The color drained from her face as she covered her mouth.

"Maray, are you going to be sick?" I asked calmly.

She nodded.

I helped her back to her seat, grabbing a trash can and positioning it at her feet. She leaned forward, elbows on knees, and I held the back of her neck, happy to have a reason to touch her.

"Why can't you just let me go?" she moaned without looking up.

I forced myself to take my hand off her.

"That's not how our program works."

She buried her face in her hands. "I'm such an idiot. Such an idiot..." she kept saying.

"I'm going to get you some water. That should help you feel a little better."

As soon as I was outside the room, I walked up to the guys.

"Well, what do you think?" I asked.

"Dude, you made her sick. Literally," Nico said, laughing.

"Looks like you've got her. You've already won

round one," Colt said, pressing some money into my hand.

"Wait, guys. I think we can make this really interesting. What we'll do is make bets on each of the tasks—whether or not she'll complete them, and how well she does."

A smile lit up Dom's face. "Dude, that's brilliant."

"Awesome. I'll have Delphine take everyone's bets."

Nico rubbed his hands together with glee. That's how he was. "What's the buy-in, gentlemen? And we're not talking pussy bets, here."

Dom shrugged. "Okay, big mouth. How about a quarter million apiece?"

Jesus.

"That would be a million-dollar pot," Colt said.

"Wow. Look at the math guy over there," Nico chided.

"Look, guys. I need to get Maray some water."

Nico was watching Maray shake her head and mumble to herself. "This is gonna be great," he said.

Colt held one hand up. "Hey, before you go, Leo, we need to talk about the Russians."

Shit. The Russians.

"What are they up to now?" I asked.

You never knew with them.

"They... have some requests to make of us."

I could just imagine. The Russians had come to New York well after the Italian mobsters but stormed the place like they owned it. Talk about bad blood. And they never seemed to learn their lesson, no matter how many times we smacked them down.

"Jesus. What the hell do they want now?"

Dom cracked his neck. "They want you to stop extending credit to players. They say it makes it harder for them to do business."

Fuckers. Of course it was hard for them to do business. Because their business *sucked*.

"It's their fucking problem if they don't want to extend credit. If players prefer our club, that's their choice. We're not holding a gun to anyone's head, and if the Russians can't compete, nothing we can do about it. Those fuckers have a lot of nerve, trying to tell us how to run our business."

Now I was in a shit mood. And I still had to deal with Maray. Goddammit.

Dom nodded. "Sounds good. I'll get the message back to them."

I looked down at my thousand-dollar wing tips. "Hold on. It's been a long time since we've met with them. If they seem upset by our stance, set something up, okay? Something face-to-face."

"Yeah, man. I'm on it."

Christ. The last thing I felt like dealing with were pissed-off Russians. But we couldn't and wouldn't cave to their demands. First, that would set a dangerous precedent, letting them dictate how we ran our business, and second, we just plain weren't dicks to our players. We *partnered* with them. If they needed bridge loans or what have you, we tried to help them out. It kept them loyal. Very loyal.

It was part of what made our card club so successful and made my business partners and me a shit ton of money.

I had better things to think about than the Russians across town. Like the beautiful college coed I was about to have a lot of fun with, and who was going to earn me a lot of money.

Dom, Nico, and Colt would never know what hit them.

10

MARAY

HOW IN THE hell was I to know that stealing something worth more than five hundred dollars was a freaking *felony*?

But if I'd known, would it have deterred me anyway?

Nah.

Not that I was an expert or anything, but speaking for myself, I didn't steal that bag thinking I was going to be caught. It's like that filter, the one that might say *don't do it—it's against the law,* just disappeared from my consciousness for a few seconds, or at least long enough to place something in my shopping bag without paying for it.

But it sure looked like I was going to pay for it now,

and as far as I could tell, to the tune of way more than the eight-hundred-dollar price tag on it.

That silky, pale pink evening bag with the secret compartment.

The one that made me feel worthy of… well, everything I wanted to be, until the dastardly Leo Borroni had grabbed me by the arm and dragged me out of Saks.

I figure the joy had lasted all of three seconds.

He'd wasted no time. In fact, the bastard must have been watching me to pounce like he had.

The thought made my skin crawl.

How long did it take to decide you hated someone?

I barely knew him but was pretty sure I did. At least I was trying to. Really hard. I wasn't one, at least not usually, to have any sort of attraction to the thug type of guy. But this one, the fucker who was trying to ruin my life, sure was managing to get under my skin. I was trying my hardest to resist him and send him packing by being the biggest bitch I could. But it didn't seem to be working.

The more I saw of him, the more I *wanted* to see of him.

And the meaner I was to him, the happier he seemed.

Bastard.

He operated in a world completely foreign to me—fake-arresting people, limos and drivers, high-stakes poker games—I was in so far over my head it wasn't funny.

The door to my little cell—Leo had called it an 'interview room'—flew open, scaring the crap out of me.

"Sorry, Maray. Didn't mean to startle you."

Remain calm.

"It's all right. I was lost in thought, I guess," I said breezily, as if I were locked in rooms with handsome men all the time.

He sat opposite me, and damn if he didn't smell good. Nothing fancy—no cologne or anything like that —just clean man. And the expression he wore on his face ran tingles up my spine. It was a sort of smirk that wasn't completely offensive or dickish, but more of a half-smile marked permanently on his face. I didn't get the feeling he was mocking me but rather just being nice. Like trying to make me feel comfortable in a weird-ass situation.

Wait. Was he *flirting* with me?

He handed me my water. "Maray, why did you steal the purse?"

Not sure I owed him an explanation.

"Why? Why do you care? You just want me to play your weird game," I said.

He shrugged. "You don't have to tell me. I was just curious, really."

Was I laying on the bitch act too thick?

"All right. My sorority has a formal coming up, and

I was able to borrow a dress from another girl. But, I needed a bag to go with it. Pretty simple, really."

It had started out simple, anyway.

He studied me, puzzled. "But why something so high-end? I mean, surely they have evening bags at Macy's."

Good question.

I looked down at my chipped DIY manicure. "I guess I wanted something fancy, something my sorority sisters would envy or admire."

I may as well just admit it. I cared what those bitches thought. It was the ugly, pathetic, sad truth. And something about my saying it out loud changed Leo's expression.

The man probably felt sorry for me, now. Thought I was a huge loser.

So I figured I'd capitalize on my disadvantage.

"So you see, Leo, that's why I'm hoping you'll just let me go. I had a temporary lapse in judgment and let pride get the better of me. I don't know why I care what those bitchy girls think, or why I felt the need to impress them. It was a mistake. A big mistake."

And just when I thought I was wearing him down, he shook his head. "I'm sorry, but I can't let you go. For one, my business partners are watching us talk right now. They've taken bets on the outcome of our conversation." He gestured at the giant mirror spanning one wall.

Um, what?

"There are people on the other side of that mirror?" I asked quietly.

He nodded.

What. The. Fuck.

My face got hot. Really hot. "You're kidding me. Like you haven't done enough already to humiliate me? Now you have people *watching* me go through this bullshit? You and your *business partners* are having fun at my fucking expense? I'm the entertainment?" My voice grew louder with each word, and now I was standing, screaming right into the asshole's face.

Not surprisingly, he was completely untroubled by my outburst. Like I said, I was in *way* over my head with these people.

"That's it. Just take me back to Saks. I'll pay for my crime and be done with you and your thug friends."

He pressed his lips together, I could swear to suppress a laugh. Fucker.

"And you people over there, watching me. Go *fuck yourselves!*" I screamed and threw my glass of water against the mirror. The tumbler shattered and water flew, but the mirror remained intact.

It was probably bulletproof or some shit like that.

Leo sighed. "If that's what you prefer, then that's what we'll do. But there's one more thing I'd like you to consider."

I stood, looking at him, hands on my hips.

"How will it feel for your parents to know what you've done?"

Shit.

He had me.

I sank back into my chair, glaring at his perfect face. God I wish I could have smacked the handsome off it.

I'd just fucked up my entire life. Regardless of whether I was going to be arrested at Saks or had to commit the petty crimes Leo and his friends were extorting me to, I was ruined.

He looked at his watch and stood. "C'mon. Let's get going. I'll have my driver take us back to Saks, where you'll be charged with grand larceny."

Did he just say *grand larceny*?

I was going to be charged with grand larceny?

He opened the door to the room and walked out.

"Wait," I called.

I heard a loud sigh, and he turned, standing in the doorway. "What? C'mon. You're wasting my time."

"I'll do it."

11

MARAY

LEO HAD CERTAINLY DONE a three-sixty when I'd caved and told him I'd play his game. A smile crept across his face, and he introduced me to his business partners—Dom, Nico, and Colt were their names, all very good-looking guys in their own right, but none quite as beautiful as Leo. Damn him.

I knew these guys. I mean, I didn't *know* them, but I knew their type. Young masters of the universe who wore bespoke suits, went to the most exclusive night-clubs, and drank whatever expensive whiskey was in fashion at the moment.

And, apparently, one of their favorite pastimes was placing bets on idiots like me who had little or no choice in joining their folly. Taking advantage of people in a bind, that's what they did for fun. Or even *putting* them in a bind so they had no choice but to play.

But I got that it was better than being charged with grand larceny. Actually, I wasn't even sure what grand larceny was, but it sure didn't sound like anything I wanted to be acquainted with, up close or personal. Or even from a distance. No thanks.

After introductions had been made outside the interview room, and the guys gleefully welcomed me to their little betting game as if I'd had a choice about it, Leo had Smitt take me home.

"I'll be in touch, Maray." He hesitated, then turned on his heel and headed down the hall.

To his office?

Or was he going back to Saks to look for another idiot shoplifter like myself?

Smitt put his hand on my arm. "Right this way," he said, leading me to the elevator I'd exited not long before.

What a difference an hour could make.

I'd been scared to death, wondering how I was going to survive a kidnapping. Now I was free to go.

Smitt opened the back door of the car they'd picked me up in, and I jumped in. They'd been kind enough to return my backpack to me, but I wasn't sure what had happened to the handbag. I figured I'd follow up on that later—if I was going through all this trouble, you'd better be damn sure that bag was going to come home with me at some point.

We drove across Manhattan, my head leaning against the cool window glass. Jesus, what had just happened? I absentmindedly smoothed my hand over the expensive leather back seat and came in contact with a cold piece of metal and some paper.

I looked to find a money clip bearing the initials *LB* stuffed with hundred-dollar bills. It must have slipped out of Leo's pocket when he was trying to get me out of the car.

"Is this the right place, Maray?" Smitt asked, pulling over and snapping me out of my thoughts.

"Yes." I stuffed the money clip and bills into my pocket. If I was facing a life of crime, why not get started on it now?

"Hey, Smitt, would you mind taking me to the end of the block?"

He nodded and smiled. "No problem."

Last thing I needed was for anyone I knew to start asking me questions about why I was getting rides in a limo when I was supposed to be finishing my shift at Bagelry.

Damn. They were probably going to fire my ass for being a no-show. Mel had no tolerance for unreliable students, and I was already on his shit list for being late all the time.

After I got home, I headed straight to my room, where I locked the door and kept the lights turned out. I was pretty sure no one had seen me come in, but if someone had, I was armed and ready with a fake migraine story should someone insist on chatting me up.

I was not in a chatty mood.

I stripped down to my panties, pulled on a ratty T-shirt, and crawled into bed where I hoped I could stay for, oh, maybe the next couple years?

What the fuck had just happened to me?

I had never been so happy to be home. I burrowed under the down comforter my roommate had given me for my birthday the year before and took deep breaths, trying to calm myself. I'd been in difficult situations before and always muddled my way through. I'd figure this one out.

Actually, fuck those guys. Instead of relaxing, anger began to well through me, even though I couldn't wipe Leo's gorgeous face from my mind.

How dare they set me up like they had? Assholes. I wasn't falling for their bullshit. They couldn't make me do anything I didn't want to. If push came to shove, I'd just deny stealing the purse, although I was pretty sure that would be futile.

It's funny, the energy that being pissed off creates. I jumped out of bed, flicked on the lights, and pulled on my most comfy sweats. I wasn't going to hide.

I popped down the hall to Lulu and Aimee's room. They were pretty much always there. They hardly ever went to class and prided themselves on being rail thin, so rarely made an appearance at meals. The only time they really went out was to go shopping or clubbing.

"Maray!" Lulu said, looking up from painting her nails. "Where are my bagels, girl?"

How girls who survived on bagels stayed so skinny was beyond me.

"Sorry. They were all out."

Aimee's gaze snapped up from her laptop. "What?"

I nodded sadly. "Yup. All sold out. Can you believe it?"

She went back to her laptop.

"Hey, aren't you home early? And whose car was that I saw you getting out of?" Lulu demanded.

Damn.

"You saw me getting out of a car?" I asked innocently.

She nodded. "Yeah, I was looking out the window and saw you at the end of the block."

"Oh. Right. Well, Mel decided to close early and hired a car to take me and the other girls home."

Lulu looked at me like I was full of shit, which, of course, I was. Not only was I a lousy thief, I was also a lousy liar.

She shrugged and dropped it, occupied by more important things. "Anyway... what's up with the formal? Have we invited the *right* people?"

I knew exactly what she meant. She wanted the fraternity with the hottest guys on campus at the party, just like we all did. But she was obsessed with it.

"Um, yeah, I mean I think they're coming. I gotta confirm."

She narrowed her eyes at me. "Maray, you wanted to run this formal, even though we didn't think you had the experience. It's up to you to get the right guys there."

Normally, I would have backed down to her. But I'd already had about all the shit I could handle for one day.

"Relax, Lulu," I snapped. "It will be taken care of."

Her eyes widened. "Well, look who's getting huffy."

"I'm not huffy—"

"Ladies, I plan to finish what I started with that guy at our last party," Aimee said, cutting me off.

Lulu rolled her eyes. "God, Aimee, you're always on your knees. Give it a break."

Her eyes flared. "Fuck off, Lulu. At least I don't take it up the ass on the first date."

Oh. Shit.

"What about you, Maray?" Aimee asked sweetly.

Damn. Just when I was trying to sneak out of their room.

"Huh? What do you mean? What about me?" I asked.

She laughed, dropping her head back. "Do you take it up the ass on the first date?"

Was she serious?

"Oh. Well, no. I mean… no. I don't do that. Sort of thing."

I didn't tell them I'd only ever been with one guy, who unfortunately could barely find my vagina. When he did, he had no idea what to do with it. I mean, I was fine with sucking face and letting a guy feel me up, but I wasn't getting down and dirty with just anyone like some of my sorority sisters did. And I didn't do the ass thing so many of them loved talking about.

Lulu and Aimee looked at each other, shrugged, and went back to what they'd been doing before I'd arrived.

My signal to leave.

But just as I did, Lulu hollered after me, "Don't forget, Maray, we're counting on you…"

Yeah. I had more important things on my mind at that moment than making sure Aimee had a dick to suck and Lulu was getting her anal fix.

As if my day hadn't already been bizarre enough.

12

LEO

SMITT and I pulled up in the Town Car just in time to see Maray leaving her building with a bunch of other girls.

They were a beautiful lot, all wearing the college uniform of skinny jeans and sneakers. But even though they were dressed alike, they were anything but ordinary.

You could see it in the way they walked.

Several of them, like Maray, were chatting as they hustled to class. But some of the others floated. Not a care in the world.

I knew that type.

They were beautiful, popular, and from well-off families. They didn't have a care in the world. They squeaked by with good-enough grades, their dads paid their bills, and they had guys knocking their doors down. Privilege spilled out of their pores.

And this was who Maray had been trying to keep up with.

Who was whispering in her ear, encouraging her along a path that culminated in stealing?

"Maray," I yelled out the car window as Smitt pulled up alongside the group.

She spun around, as they all did, and I had to say, she was more beautiful than any of them. Her perfect, clear complexion was washed with pink in the morning cold, and wisps of blonde hair that had escaped her ponytail whipped around in the breeze.

A couple of them smiled, and the others looked from me, to Maray, and then back to me again, whispering, nudging, and giggling.

"Maray, looks like someone wants to talk to you," a brunette chided, giving her a little shove toward my car.

Maray frowned and said something to her friends, and made her way over to my open window. The crowd on the sidewalk remained frozen in place.

"What are you doing here?" Maray asked quietly, frowning as she leaned toward the open window. "Now you're a stalker, as well as a kidnapper?"

I opened the car door for her and scooted over to make room for her in the backseat. "Picking you up. We have work to do." I waved her in.

But she shook her head. "I have class. Sorry." She

turned and started jogging to catch up with her friends, who'd started walking again but not without looking over their shoulders.

"Maray, if I were you, I'd get in the car," I called.

She sighed and waved at the group. "I'll catch up with you guys later," she grumbled and hopped in.

"Morning, Maray," Smitt said cheerfully.

"Morning," she mumbled, glaring at me. "What the hell are you doing here, and why did I need to get in your car? What kind of *work* do we have to do?"

"Kiss me first," I said. "Give them something to really talk about."

She rolled her eyes, leaning toward me and giving me a peck on the cheek.

Getting under this beautiful woman's skin could become my favorite new pastime.

"Who were they, those women? Your sorority friends?" I asked.

Smitt sped up, passing the group, all of whom continued to stare until we were out of sight.

"Yeah. That's them."

"Are they nice? Good people?"

I already knew the answer, but wanted to hear her say it.

She gave me a long look before responding. "In another life, I'm not sure I'd hang out with most of them. But it is what it is right now, at least until I graduate. I guess they'll be good contacts to have after college."

I scoffed. I couldn't help it. "I guess they're good contacts, if you want to get into the country club or volunteer for a charity. But most of those women are not going to be the kind of mover and shaker you will be."

Now it was her turn to scoff. "Is that what you think? How would you know?"

I looked out the window at the gray New York morning. "I see it in you. The hunger."

"You don't even know me," she said, without missing a beat.

It was true.

I nodded. "I don't know you well. But I know a few things."

She pressed her lips together. "Whatever. But now I'm missing class, which is not a huge deal because today was just a review session. However, my shift at Bagelry starts just afterwards. Can you drive me there? Or are we supposed to ride around and chat all day?"

I watched her trying to get mad as her posture stiffened and she avoided my gaze.

I leaned over the seat toward Smitt. "Hey, can you take us over to Bagelry?"

He nodded.

Maray's head snapped in my direction. "Thank you. I appreciate the ride."

"Oh, I'm not dropping you off. You're just running in to tell your boss you quit."

She shook her head, then buried her face in her

hands. "Oh my god. Are you kidding? Are you just trying to ruin every aspect of my life?"

I recognized the dramatic tendencies someone picks up from spending too much time with spoiled rich girls.

"*Ruin* your life. That's an interesting perspective."

"Really? It sure as hell doesn't look like you're trying to *enhance* it. First, you want to turn me in to Saks. Then you and your friends bet on how far I'll go with your stupid dares. Now, you're not only making me miss class, but also quit my job, which I'm *required to have* under the terms of my scholarship. It's called *work study*. Ever heard of it?"

Oh, to kiss the anger right off her face. But there'd be time for that.

We pulled up in front of Bagelry, one of those hipster places where they put shit like avocado on your pineapple-flavored bagel.

I nodded toward the door. "Go ahead. I'll wait."

"I can't just quit," she said, her voice beginning to tremble.

I reached for her hand, which, surprisingly, she didn't pull back. Was she... curious about me?

I nodded toward the shop. "Go on. It's part of the deal you made with us. And don't worry, you won't get in trouble with the school. Everything will be taken care of."

She frowned, grabbed her backpack, and slammed the car door behind herself.

Smitt looked at me in the rearview mirror. "You're really leaning on her."

I respected Smitt's opinion. I really did. He'd been with my family for a long time and had come to New York with me from Vegas when I'd needed a change. I knew his leaving was a big loss for my brother, who also really depended on him, but we'd agreed New York wasn't intended to be forever.

It had its ups and downs, no doubt. What place didn't?

Annoying people, and great people. Beautiful women, and crazy women. Amazing business opportunities, and lots of ways to lose your shirt. Not that Vegas was that different—it just wasn't as extreme. And it didn't get as fucking cold.

I looked at him in the rearview mirror. "Hey, can you turn up the heat? And yeah, I know I'm putting the screws to her. It's part of the program. Gotta break her down to build her up."

Smitt sighed. "All right, man. You know what you're doing."

The car door flew open, and Maray got in, slamming it and locking it behind her.

What the fuck?

She fumbled through her backpack, pulled out a tissue, and sniffled.

"So?" I asked.

If someone had hurt her… well, it wasn't going to be pretty.

"Um… well… Mel just screamed at me. I mean, he's an asshole, but I just didn't expect that."

To my surprise, she gazed directly at me with her wet eyes, as if she needed comforting.

But I wasn't good at that kind of shit.

"What did he say?"

Smitt pulled into traffic.

"Oh, just that I was a stupid unreliable little bitch—"

My heart slammed against my chest, and I crunched my hands into painful fists. "Seriously? The owner of a bagel shop spoke to you that way?"

I didn't like getting pissed off. I tried to avoid it. It never ended well.

She nodded, shaking her head and looking out the car window.

I looked over the back seat toward Smitt. "Did you hear that? The bagel guy called Maray a bitch."

He nodded. "Not a good move."

I took a deep breath. "We'll take care of him later."

"What does that mean?" Maray asked.

"You'll see."

13

LEO

"See that newspaper vendor over there?" I asked, pointing to a little kiosk surrounded by crumpled-up newspaper, food containers, and other trash.

Smitt pulled over, a safe distance from our target.

Maray craned her neck, more blonde hair spilling from her ponytail. "Yes. What about it?"

"He's a pig. He leaves his unsold papers out at night and lets them blow down the street."

She turned to me. "Really? He doesn't just put them in the garbage? What a jerk."

"Like I said, he's a pig. I've been watching him do this for a long time."

"Okay. So why are you telling me this?"

I smiled. "You're going to teach him a lesson."

"What? Me?" she asked, pointing at herself.

I nodded. "Yup. This is what we're going to do."

I explained that Smitt and I would wait at the other end of the block, where we could watch her approach the vendor. She was to confront him about his trash, and when he told her to stuff it, as he undoubtedly would, she was to grab his stack of *New York Times* and run.

"Are you fucking kidding me?" she asked. "That's the dumbest thing I've ever heard."

Smitt slowly drove us around the block and idled the car where we'd have a clear view of her encounter.

In spite of her protest, I reached to open her car door. "Go ahead," I said, gesturing. "Newspaperman awaits."

She shook her head, frowning. "I can't steal his newspapers—"

I put my finger to her lips. "You can, and you will. Go."

She got out of the car and slowly approached the vendor, rubbing her hands on her thighs and looking around.

"Think she'll do it?" Smitt asked.

I watched her get closer to the kiosk, where she pretended to browse.

"Yeah. This is easy shit," I laughed. "She's just getting warmed up. Or should I say, we're just getting her warmed up."

She started speaking, gesturing at the trash on the ground.

"How much you got riding on it?" Smitt asked.

"A million. Two-fifty from each of us."

He whistled quietly. "You guys are crazy."

No doubt. You had to be crazy to be in the business we were in, setting up card games for high rollers. It was not without its risks. Big risks, depending on the day.

But that's how we guys rolled. We loved our risks. And, of course, betting. We'd bet on fucking anything. I once lost a thousand dollars betting that it wouldn't snow exactly two inches. And don't you know, it snowed exactly two inches.

The vendor looked around at the trash Maray had pointed out, waved his hands as New Yorkers do, and gave a *not my problem* shrug.

But Maray didn't give up. I had to hand it to her, she was sticking it to him. With her hands on her hips, she shook her head. I didn't need to hear the conversation to know exactly what was going on.

The vendor, in defiance, pulled himself up to full height, which still left him a couple inches shorter than Maray—a fact that probably drove him crazy. He shook a finger in her face.

She crossed her arms over her chest and looked down, shaking her head. She pointed at his unsold stack of *New York Times*, which he was probably about to sell a shit ton of during the upcoming lunch rush hour, and bent to pick one up.

The man smiled, probably thinking he'd gotten a

sale out of his tree-hugging, trash-hating customer, but his smile quickly faded when he saw what she did next.

It couldn't have been easy, but Maray scooped up the stack of twenty-five or so newspapers, turned, and started running. Smitt put the car in drive, and I opened the door for her to pile in. With her stolen goods, of course.

The man was right on her tail, screaming and attracting the attention of everyone on the sidewalk. But Maray was faster, and as soon as she'd gotten in the car with the papers, Smitt screeched down the street.

She leaned her head back and closed her eyes, still clutching the bundle of papers. "Oh my god. Oh my god. I just stole newspapers," she said, out of breath.

She'd stolen other things as well, but I didn't bother to point that out.

"Good work," I said, patting her on the leg.

She exhaled and turned to me excitedly. "He was such as asshole, completely unapologetic about the mess he was creating. He kept saying there was nothing he could do about it when I pointed out a trash can not twenty feet away. Then, he called me a bitch. Second time today I've been called that. I kind of snapped."

Perfect.

"Think he'll learn his lesson?" I asked.

She shifted the papers onto the seat between us and looked at her newsprint-stained fingers. "I guess we'll see."

I knew she'd handle this easily.

"What are we doing with all these papers?" she asked.

Smitt looked at her in the rearview mirror. "We're going to drop them off."

She looked between the two of us. "We are? Where?"

I looked out the window at the building Smitt had just pulled up to. "Right here."

"Here?" she asked.

I loved the wrinkles on her forehead when she frowned. She reminded me of... well, it wasn't time to think about that.

"Go ahead," I said, waving my arm.

"What is this? An old folks home?"

I nodded.

She took a deep breath and scooped the papers back into her arms. She ran up the steps of St. Mary's Home for the Aged.

When she jumped back in the car, her cheeks were flushed and her face was covered in a grin. "They were very appreciative. All those cute old people now get free newspapers. You should have seen them. I feel a little like Robin Hood."

"Oh yeah? And to think you're just getting started."

14

LEO

"You want mustard?" I asked, handing Maray the two dogs she'd ordered from a street vendor.

She nodded and held them to me as I covered her lunch in the yellow stuff. Then I turned back to the vendor and grabbed my own dogs, doused in relish.

I loved how when I asked if she wanted lunch, she pointed to a street vendor.

"Do your sorority sisters know you eat hot dogs from a vendor?" I asked as we walked around the block.

She looked up at me, a smudge of mustard in the corner of her mouth. "Hell no."

"Why do you do this to yourself?"

Her head whipped in my direction. "Do what?"

I stopped walking to face her. "Pressure yourself to keep up."

Surprise crossed her face.

I wanted to tell her how easy it was to see she was pretending to be someone she wasn't, but why insult her? People had to learn shit on their own. Make their own mistakes.

Just ask me.

She sighed. "I had a guidance counselor who told me this was the way to do things. That if I played my cards right, my future would fall into place. You know —go to the right school, meet the right people, act the right way."

"Sounds like a real winner. And how's that working out for you?"

She stiffened, then suddenly looked at her watch. "I have to get ready for class."

Okay. She wasn't ready to face facts. But it was all good. I was drawn to her in a way I hadn't been drawn to a woman in a long time. We'd be spending plenty of time together in the near future, so there was no need to rush anything, including important conversations.

"Maray, I have an offer for you. I need help at the card games a couple nights a week."

She shook her head. "Nah. That's not my thing. I'll get another job somewhere else."

I hooked a finger under her chin. I might have been pushing it, but I couldn't help myself. "Look, you get paid in tips. You'll walk out of there with at least a thousand bucks every night you work."

That might have gotten her.

Something washed over her—first fear, then curiosity—as she did the math in her head.

She could use the money, we both knew, but hell, I wasn't inviting her to hang around because I was a nice guy. I wanted to see more of her, plain and simple. And to make sure she felt the same way about me.

Which she would, in time. I could be patient when I had to.

There was something about her that was scrappy. Sure, she might have been more sheltered than most women I knew, but she had drive.

And, she was sexy in a completely unselfconscious way, which was the best kind of sexy. She didn't even try, with her jeans, sneakers, and little or no makeup— she was a natural beauty. Very different from the typical woman I was attracted to, but hey, maybe it was time to turn over a new leaf.

She bit her bottom lip while thinking of what to say about my offer. I waited patiently. I knew her well enough to know she couldn't be pushed.

"I don't know," she said softly, shaking her head over her conflicted thoughts. "I mean, is that stuff even legal?"

I was hoping she'd ask. "It's a complex business, but yes, the way we do it is legal."

She frowned. "What do you do to make it legal?"

"In a nutshell, it's legal as long as the house—that means me and my business partners—don't take a *rake*."

"A rake?"

"That's a cut of the money played in each hand. If that goes to anyone other than the players, like if we took it for the club, that would be illegal. We also keep no cash on the premises."

Her eyes widened. "How do you make money, then?"

"You really are a finance major, aren't you?" I said, laughing. "We make money by selling memberships to the club."

She nodded slowly. "And how do you play with no cash?"

"We use wires. Everyone wires the money they need to buy in and then to cover any losses. Then, the winners get their money via wires, too. There's a trust factor. That's why we do background checks and inter- view people who want to join."

I didn't bother telling her how we also extended credit to certain, qualified members, much to the chagrin of our Russian competitors. That was more detail than she needed.

"Holy shit. A whole world out there I know nothing of."

After our hotdogs, I walked her to class. "Don't feel badly. Most people know nothing about high-stakes poker. There's really no reason to, unless you're going to play. And to play, you need to have a fuckload of money."

When we reached her classroom door, I stopped. "What do you think?"

"Well. I do need a new job."

15

MARAY

A COUPLE DAYS LATER, I scooted into my senior Econ class at the last minute so I could avoid anyone I knew, and grabbed a seat in the back of the room so I could be the first out.

The instructor, who I usually enjoyed, was droning on about something the Federal Reserve had done, but I couldn't focus. I'd normally geek out on the minutiae of the country's money supply, but for some reason it suddenly seemed ridiculously obscure. And unimportant.

I never thought I'd say that.

'Course I never thought I'd be a newspaper stealing vigilante, either.

But the harder I stared at the blank notebook page before me, the more clearly I saw Leo's face.

Before he'd nabbed me in Saks, I hadn't known someone like him even existed. I mean, sure, he was gorgeous and all with those dark eyes, thick black hair, and chiseled jawline, but there was an air about him that made me shake when he was near.

Had he noticed? God, I hoped not.

He was more than the quintessential alpha dude. Yes, he was brimming with confidence and authority, but he also had an air about him that let you know you were going do whatever he said, whether you wanted to or not.

It was like a spell, that's what it was. And it was beyond hot.

I knew I could fight Leo and his plans for me as much as I wanted, but in the end I was putty in his hands. And I was pretty sure he knew that. Guys like that always knew how powerful they were, gliding through life, opening doors with scarcely an effort. He was privileged in the way my sorority sisters were. He'd walk into a room like he owned it and leave with everyone in his pocket.

I guess you called that charisma.

And I was afraid he was about to charm the pants right off me. He'd not made any passes at me, per se, but the way he looked at me—well, more than once I wanted to throw myself at him and let him have his way.

Jesus, I sounded like a dog in heat. But I guess guys like Leo will do that.

Lucky them.

And lucky me. Maybe.

And he wanted to give me a job? What the hell was that all about? I didn't know anything about high-stakes poker. I didn't know anything about poker, period, except you needed chips and cards. And money.

And what exactly did he need me to do, especially for tips of a thousand bucks a night?

I closed my notebook, slipped on my jacket, and grabbed my backpack to sneak out of class. I wasn't getting anything out of the lecture, and I desperately needed to clear my head. And just as I walked out of class, I ran right into one of my sorority sisters.

Crap.

"Hey, you!" Weeza cried.

Her real name was Louisa, but she'd always insisted on being called by her nickname. She thought it was cute. What she didn't know was that half the girls in the sorority called her 'Knees-a,' because she reportedly spent so much time on her knees giving blowjobs to frat boys.

"Hi, Weez. What's up?"

She looked like a snow bunny, overdressed for the cool-but-not-cold day, wearing a white down puffer trimmed in thick raccoon fur, and Ugg boots.

She smiled liked we shared a secret. "Who was that guy who picked you up earlier? The one in the Town Car with the driver?"

"Oh, no one," I shrugged.

But I should have known that wouldn't get rid of her. Weeza loved her gossip. "Are you keeping secrets from us, Mar? How'd you meet a guy like that?" With a hand on her hip and confusion on her face, it was clear she thought Leo was out of my league.

I mean, he was. But what a bitch to point it out.

I was tempted to tell her I'd met Leo when shoplifting an eight-hundred-dollar evening bag to impress her and the rest of the sorority, but it sounded so outlandish I doubted she'd even believe it.

I could hardly believe it, myself.

"I met him at that club we went to last month. Remember?" I lied, hoping she didn't.

Thinking, she scrunched up her face, then slowly shook her head. "Wasn't that when you left early? You got your period or something?"

God, she had a good memory. I actually hadn't gotten my period. I'd just wanted to get the hell out of there.

"Yeah, but on my way out, he chatted me up and asked for my number," I said as matter-of-factly as I could.

She wasn't buying a word I was saying.

"So, what's his name?" she asked.

"Leo. Leo Borroni."

I could see she was running his name through her head as if she might somehow know him. "Are ya bringing him to the formal?"

Shit. The formal.

"Doubt it. I'm interested in that other guy, Thomas."

She nodded slowly, trying to assess just how much I might be full of shit. "Right. Thomas. I think he's going out with Lulu now."

Whatever.

I smiled brightly. "Guess I'll be going alone, then. We can hang out together!" I slapped her on the back before sauntering away.

"Um. Yeah. Maybe," she called after me.

Fuck off, bitch.

I tucked my hair down the back of my jacket and pulled my hood up. I wasn't cold. I just wanted to disappear. Have some anonymity. I wasn't sure the hood on my jacket would accomplish that for me, but it felt safe and cozy, if only for a moment.

Still a few blocks from my apartment, I rounded the corner, lost in thought. Actually, I wasn't completely lost in thought. I was rubbing my hand, the one that Leo had brushed in the car. At the time, I'd suppressed it as best I could, but an electric jolt had shot down my spine when he'd touched me. His hand was large—huge actually— dwarfing mine, and it was warm, like a cozy sleeping blanket. I wanted to give him mine to warm up, since they were always cold. But I didn't.

And what was the deal with that Smitt guy? Was he security? Or just a driver? Did he carry a gun?

And more importantly, could I introduce him to one of my sorority sisters? A burly, rugged guy like him? They'd be all over his ass. Literally.

But that wouldn't be appropriate. I needed to fulfill my obligation to Leo, whatever the hell that meant, and get on with my life. He'd forget me and be on to the next girl he could extort into playing his weird fucking betting game.

I stopped in my tracks when I realized that in my aimless wandering, I had no idea where I was. I checked out the street sign and found I was on Sixth Avenue, exactly where I should have been.

Then why did it look so unfamiliar?

Because Bagelry was gone. The little shop, my former place of employment, which I always walked by to and from class, was *gone*. Just gone. Brown paper covered the inside of the windows, and the awning with the shop's name had been sloppily painted over. The benches that had been out front had been pulled from their bolts, and there was a big chain and padlock on the door.

Holy shit. Just two days earlier, the place had been humming with business.

As I stood gawking at the closed store, two other college students walked up. "What happened to Bagelry?" one asked.

I shook my head. "No idea. They're just gone."

He looked at his buddy, and they scratched their heads. "Damn shame. Their bagels were killer."

With a second glance, I recognized them as regular customers whom I'd waited on many times. I pulled my hood more tightly around my face and kept walking.

Digging my hands deep in my pockets, I found the money clip and cash I'd discovered in Leo's car. I'd forgotten all about it. And even though I'd give it back eventually, I got a kick out of hanging on to it. It gave me some power. Like I had *one up* on him.

He might make me jump around like a little puppet, but I had his money.

Some of it, anyway.

16

MARAY

ANOTHER COUPLE DAYS WENT BY, and no Leo. I'd taken his money out of my jacket pocket and stuffed it into a ratty old rain boot in the back of my closet. As much as my sorority sisters liked to help themselves to each other's clothes, no one would ever lower themselves to using my decidedly uncool rain boots. Which was fine. I might not have stylish or expensive stuff, but at least no one touched it. For the most part.

Except that one time.

My parents, as an early graduation gift, had bought me a beautiful interview suit at Ann Taylor. I'd tried it on umpteen times, and it fit perfectly. I felt like I could, if not conquer the world in it, then at least get any job I really wanted.

And then, one day, I'd come home from class and

walked right into one of my sorority sisters returning from dinner out with her parents.

Wearing my suit. The new one. That I'd never worn.

What. The. Fuck.

That's right. She was wearing my brand-new interview suit. The one that was going to take me far into the reaches of a successful New York career in finance. The one I was going to use until the darn thing wore out at the seams.

It was also the one that had been a stretch for my parents to afford. The one they'd put on their credit card, which they never did except in cases of emergencies.

There was no being nice that day.

I lost my shit and screamed at her until she took the pants and jacket off right there in the hallway. I'd gathered them up, ran to my room, slammed the door so hard the frame chipped, and stuffed the whole bundle into a dark corner in the back of my closet.

My excitement over the suit was ruined. Completely and totally ruined. Of course I'd dry-clean it at some point, and still wear it someday, but at that moment, the suit represented every disappointment I'd ever had in my life.

I'd finally gotten something nice, and some inconsiderate shit whose parents could probably buy her ten suits had tainted it. Destroyed it, really. At least that's what I'd thought at the time.

Maybe I was overreacting. Maybe I was being a brat. I didn't care.

That was the last time anyone helped themselves to anything in my closet.

With the mystery of the shuttered Bagelry weighing on me, I headed straight home and sneaked into my room without anyone noticing. For the most part, I liked living with my sorority sisters, but sometimes I just didn't want to talk to anyone. Those times were tough. We were expected to be 'on' all the time. It was exhausting.

As I pulled out my Econ book to see if I could make up for the lecture I'd skipped out on, my phone vibrated.

"Hello," I said, grabbing the call when I saw it was Leo.

"Maray," he said simply.

Goddamn if his voice wasn't more delicious over the phone than even in person. It felt like warm honey being poured on my private parts, and then licked clean—

Wait.

Christ, was I turning into one of my in-heat sorority sisters? Some of them pursued nookie more than any guy I knew.

"Just opened my Econ book to read a few chapters that will hopefully make some sort of sense. Oh, by the way, I walked past Bagelry on the way home from class and... well, they're gone. Just completely closed,

And they'd been doing fine a couple days ago. It's so odd."

He cleared his throat. "Yes, I'm aware of that."

"You are?"

"I have friends, Maray, who take care of problems for me."

A shiver ran down my spine. What if *I* became a 'problem' for Leo?

"Oh... I see." I dropped my textbook and sat up, pulling my comforter tight around me.

"I can't elaborate, but let's just say your boss should have been nice to you when he had the chance. I know the building's owner."

Holy crap.

"H... how do you know the owner?" I stuttered.

He took a deep breath, and even though he was on the other end of the line, I could see his jaw shift and his Adam's apple bob. And, dammit, I was wishing he were right there in front of me.

What? I actually knew how his Adam's Apple moved?

"Leo, wow, that's kind of extreme, don't you think?"

Extreme, yes, but part of me was thrilled that Mel, the jackass owner, had got what he had coming. He could make a mean bagel, but used to treat all his employees—not just me—like crap.

I guess I felt a little shitty, too. I mean, it *was* his business.

As if he could read my mind, Leo said, "Don't feel badly, Maray. He wasn't a nice man."

Well, I wasn't the only person out of a job now. But did I want to work Leo's card games? His mention of thousand-dollar tips kept ringing in my ears.

Really loudly.

How would I explain it to my parents?

"Hey, it's nearly rush hour. Time for your next task."

What?

"Leo, I'm studying," I pleaded.

"You have a solid A in that class."

"You don't know my grades."

He sighed. "I told you, Maray. I know a lot of people."

My stomach did a couple flips. I didn't feel so well.

"Be ready in twenty minutes, Maray. Smitt and I will pick you up."

Almost true to his word, he arrived at my building twenty-*two* minutes later, and I hopped in before Smitt had fully stopped. I didn't need nosy sorority sisters asking more questions.

"Hey there," Leo said. "You look very pretty."

Were my efforts that obvious? I *had* brushed out my hair and put on some lipstick. I'll admit it. I wanted to look nice. For Leo.

"Thanks," I said breezily, looking out the car window to avoid his gaze.

We drove only two blocks before Smitt pulled over to a corner with a subway stop. "Here you go," he said.

Leo nodded at me, and we jumped out of the car on the passenger side. He scanned the crowd descending into the subway station and started walking.

I followed him down the steps, hustling to keep up. He moved through the crowd gracefully, turning his shoulders just in time to avoid colliding with a hurried commuter, sidestepping the slowpokes with ease.

When we'd gone through the gate and reached the platform, I was out of breath.

"You're a fast walker," I said.

He gave me a small smile and ran his hand up my back.

Why did I love his touch so much? He was a freaking thug. A nicely dressed and extremely handsome one, but still a thug. Look was he was forcing me to do.

Speaking of which.

I lowered my voice as the mob waiting for the train closed in. "What are we doing here, Leo? Why are we in the subway?"

He scanned the crowd as if he were looking for someone. His expression changed the slightest bit when his gaze landed on a little guy in a suit hollering into his cell phone.

"Tell that cocksucker I'm gonna tear his head off if he doesn't get that trade done..." he barked.

Nice guy.

Given that it was New York and rush hour on the subway, no one batted an eye. I'm not sure anyone around us even registered his conversation.

But Leo had.

What the hell was he up to?

He took my hand.

Christ, I was holding hands with a thug. And enjoying it.

Leo snaked through the crowd until we were right behind the loudmouth, and when the subway doors opened, we pushed in on his heels while he continued yelling into his cell.

Leo leaned toward me, and his breath on my ear caused my heart to thump against my chest. I looked down, my loose hair falling over my face so he couldn't see me blush.

But he took my face and tilted it up until I was looking at him.

"Time to get to work."

17

LEO

IN THE CRUSH of the subway, Maray was pressed against me, and while we were generally up to no good, all was right in the world. Her simple clean scent intoxicated me, and every time her freshly washed hair flew around and brushed against my face, I wanted to grab it.

With a hard tug.

Jesus. What the fuck was going on?

Down boy.

She leaned close to my ear. "What do you mean, *time to get to work*? Where are we going? And why are we on the subway?"

"You're going to steal that asshole's wallet," I whispered.

Her head snapped back, and her eyes widened in horror.

As I'd expected they would.

Her lips touched my ear. "Are you fucking kidding me?"

I nodded. "Yeah. He's a douche. And his wallet is in his jacket pocket, right here," I said, gesturing with my chin.

She followed my gaze, and found the dude's wallet was indeed ripe for the picking.

Looking back at me, she frowned. "You're crazy."

I just gestured to the guy's open pocket again, and he continued to holler at some unfortunate bastard on the other end of the line.

Probably a bad trade, judging by how he was trying to let everyone around him know he was a heavy-hitter.

Always a sure sign of someone who was *not* a heavy hitter.

We pulled into the next station, and the crowd in the car began to shift, some getting ready to disembark, and others moving out of their way.

"Do it," I growled.

She looked around, fear written all over her face. But true to New York form, no one was paying any attention to us, and certainly not the loudmouth mark I'd chosen.

"Now," I said in Maray's ear.

I jostled her, causing her to bump into the loudmouth, who looked over his shoulder and gave her a dirty look. "Watch it, lady," he growled, craning his neck to see which stop we were approaching.

Something passed over Maray's face, and I watched her slip her hand into his pocket and draw it back out.

And as she did, I jostled her against him again, in case he'd felt any movement.

But he suspected nothing and just kept jabbering about the transaction he was trying to make happen.

The subway doors opened, and the man pushed out just as Maray stuffed his wallet into her own jacket pocket.

She'd done it. Task number two was complete for my little thief.

We traveled a couple more stops and exited the train. Once back up on the street, we waited for Smitt to pick us up.

"Oh my god," Maray said, pacing, "I pickpocketed someone."

She wore a frown, which slowly morphed into a small smile and then a grin.

"You enjoyed it," I said.

She took a deep breath before she spoke. "It was a rush. So dangerous. And that man was so awful."

"Did you feel that way when you stole the purse from Saks?" I asked.

She looked at me for a minute, her lips full and glossy. "No. I didn't. I guess because taking from a store is impersonal. But this guy was such as ass."

Now she was getting it.

"So, what am I supposed to do with this thing?" she asked, patting the outside of her pocket.

"We're gonna return it."

Her eyebrows rose. "What? Then why did we take it? What was the point?"

Did she really need to ask that? I tilted my head and let her think for a moment.

Pursing her lips, she said, "Oh. Okay. I get it."

Smitt swung by and we jumped in without a word.

"Give me the wallet," I said, holding out my hand.

She placed it gingerly in my palm, as if it were dirty.

I flipped the billfold open. It was a cheap wallet, as I'd expected. Guys like him were all about show. He had a couple twenties, his license, and some credit cards, but I pulled out what I really needed.

"Here. Call him," I said, handing Maray his business card.

She scrunched up her face. Her beautiful, perfect face. "What? What do I say to him?"

"Tell him we have his wallet but that we'll be leaving it where he can easily find it."

She looked at me like I was crazy again. "You're kidding me, right? We stole his wallet just to give it right back?"

I nodded.

She sighed, snatching the card from my hand.

"Use this," I said, handing her a throwaway flip phone.

She stuffed the wallet back in her pocket and sighed, dialing the cell number featured prominently on the card. "Hello. Is this Randall?"

She looked at me and swallowed.

"Right. Randy. Hey Randy, I have your wallet—"

She nodded while his squawking voice poured out of her phone.

"Yeah. Randy, I um, I didn't actually find it. I stole it. From you."

That's my girl.

Her admission unleashed a string of obscenities on the other end of the line. I couldn't hear specifics, but it wasn't hard to figure out that the guy was losing it.

Maray raised her voice. "Randy... Randy... I'd like to get it back to you if you could shut up for just a minute."

Damn.

"I'll call you back when I know where I'm leaving it. Bye!"

She flipped the phone closed. "God, he really is a jerk. He threatened me and everything. I have half a mind to not return it to him."

"Well, that's your prerogative."

After dropping Maray at her dorm, Smitt and I returned to the card club.

"Dude, you're liking this one," he said to me from the front seat.

"I am, my friend."

He pulled into our parking garage, and we got into the elevator. "I don't blame you. She's good-looking and a sweetheart. That is, if you don't completely corrupt her," he said, laughing.

He had a point.

I walked past Colt's office and found all the guys hanging out there.

"Well, look who it is," Dom said, raising a glass to me. "The corrupter of innocent women."

Colt pressed a button on his desk, and our server appeared in seconds. "Samia, can you get Leo here a scotch?"

She smiled and nodded, disappearing as fast as she'd appeared.

I took a seat in an empty club chair, whose leather crackled as I sank in. We'd spared no expense for the place, and it had paid off. We were known for the most upscale and comfortable card club in town, which enabled us to charge our hefty membership fees.

Really hefty membership fees.

"Dude. How's your little protégé? What's her name again? Mary?" Nico asked.

Samia returned with my scotch, which I took a long draw on. God that was some good shit.

"Maray. Her name is Maray. Accent on the second

syllable," I said, knowing full well that Nico had mispronounced it on purpose.

He could be such an ass, and I could see he was just getting warmed up.

Leaning forward in his chair, he set his elbows on his knees. "You fuck her yet?"

I'd seen that coming.

"No, man," I said.

He sat back in his chair, laughing. "What are you waiting for? I mean, from what I saw that one time you brought her by, she was hot as shit. Even though she was in a hoodie and Chucks. Christ, I wonder what she'd look like all dolled up?"

Colt and Dom nodded.

"She'd be gorgeous," I said.

"So how's the bet coming? She's not playing, right? I knew she was far too straight to get into any of your shit," Colt said.

He'd been the only one to bet she'd having nothing to do with the game.

I looked at Dom and Nico, who were hoping Colt was wrong. They loved making money off the guy.

I smiled smugly. "Sorry, Colt. You're out a shit ton of money. She's completed the first two of her tasks. In fact, just an hour ago or so, she pickpocketed a guy on the subway."

Nico burst out laughing loudly enough to be heard throughout the club. "*No fucking way.* That's awesome! I bet my money she'd carry out all your shit, but I can't believe she actually did it." He leaned toward me for a big high five.

I stole a look at Dom, who'd bet that she'd accept some of the tasks, but not all. It remained to be seen whether she stuck with the program to the end, so his bet was still in the running.

But Colt had lost, that much was clear. He scowled and shrugged.

"Whatever. You assholes can have my two hundred fifty thousand," he said with a touch of bitterness.

Couldn't blame him for being pissed.

"It was a bad bet, my friend. Better luck next time."

The sour expression on his face didn't change.

"So, guys. I've offered her a job here."

All three of their heads snapped in my direction.

"You fucking kidding?" Dom asked, confusion washing across his face.

I nodded, pleased at the prospect of having her around. "I think she'll be great. With a little training, of course."

"She won't do it," Nico said. "She's not the type."

I shrugged. "Well, we'll just have to see, won't we?"

18

LEO

A COUPLE DAYS passed before I was able to get back to Maray. The holiday season was coming, and it seemed every one of our members wanted to host a private party for their poker-playing buds. It was the only time of year we permitted guests, and it was a good time to solicit new members. Of course, we had to vet those members, and that took a shitload of time.

And patience.

It was incredible how many yahoos who wanted to join the club who could not possibly afford either the membership fees or the steep buy-ins. Seriously, did these guys want to mortgage their houses and children? I knew that belonging to a card club had become *the* thing to do in Manhattan, and our club had the best reputation, but it wasn't for everyone.

"Hi, Leo," Maray said, answering my call on the first ring.

The sound of her voice soothed the hell out of me.

"How's studying?"

Her voice perked up. "Great. I got an A on my Econ exam."

I couldn't help but smile. "I know you did."

This time she didn't ask me how I knew. She was learning. The fewer questions she asked, the better off we'd all be.

"It's time to return dickhead's wallet. I'll be by in thirty minutes."

When Smitt and I arrived, I watched Maray skip down the steps of her building, but not without looking both ways to see if anyone she knew was watching.

Christ, she really did care what those sorority bitches thought of her.

We'd be working on that.

She hopped into the back seat of the car, radiating that great scent that always surrounded her. This time she'd not only done her hair and put on some lipstick, but she was also wearing boots instead of sneakers and a wool peacoat instead of a ratty hoodie.

I took that as a good sign.

"Hello, gorgeous," I said. I wasn't usually so familiar with her, but the words just came flying out of my mouth.

Don't you know she blushed to the roots of her hair. So fucking hot.

And now I was getting hard.

Focus, asshole.

"Hi, Leo. Hi, Smitt," she said.

Smitt waved over his shoulder.

"Okay. What's the address of the guy's office?" I asked.

Maray pulled the wallet out and passed me his business card.

"Smitt, head over to Fifth, okay?" I asked.

I turned back to Maray. Her proximity was making it hard to concentrate. "When we get to his office, put the wallet in one of the garbage cans outside his building. Then we'll tell him where to find it."

We pulled up and Maray looked around. "Which can? Does it matter?"

"The one over there," I said, pointing to the green mesh garbage can with no lid on it. "Near the homeless guy."

Maray started to get out but turned back to me. "Just drop it in?"

"Yup."

She was back in the car in seconds. "Now what?"

"Call him and tell him which can to look in. We'll watch."

Minutes later, as it started to drizzle, he came flying out of his building, looking around frantically. Spotting the only can with a homeless person leaning on it, he ran over.

"It's under some of the trash. He'll have to dig for it," Maray said. "It smells terrible, too."

God, I was in love.

I mean, *like*. In like.

He took a deep breath and plunged into the filthy can, rustling through newspapers, coffee cups, soiled lunch containers, and what looked to be dog poop that someone had picked up.

"I wonder if this will humble him a bit," Maray said.

"Unlikely."

He reached one more time and emerged with the wallet, opening it to make sure nothing had been taken. Then, he stuffed it in his jacket pocket.

The same pocket it had been stolen from.

But, apparently, he was not a total fool, because he rethought its placement and slipped it into his back pocket.

Before returning to his building, he looked around the plaza for a suspect. He scanned right over us in the Town Car, and headed back inside.

"Well. Good job," I said. "Now, let's head back downtown."

Smitt turned the car around until we reached a residential street in the Lower East Side. By now it was pouring rain.

"Pull over, Smitt, would you?"

He idled the car in front of some kind of hipster bar.

I handed Maray an umbrella. "See that dog over there?" I asked, pointing at a small pooch with its head bowed and tail between its legs, tied to a bike rack.

"Oh my god. That one shivering in the rain?" she asked. "Poor thing."

"Exactly. Go get him."

She looked back at me, only slightly surprised this time. "Did you just say… go get him? Like get the dog and bring him back to the car?"

"Yeah. Some fucker left him out in the rain. Let's teach them a lesson."

A smile crept across her face. "Oh my god. What a great idea." She grabbed the umbrella and darted over to the dog, untying his leash.

"C'mon, boy," she said, slapping the side of her leg.

That's all the poor thing needed. He followed her right into the car, where he jumped onto her lap and shook himself dry.

Maray burst into peals of laughter as she got soaked, and Smitt pulled away from the curb. I reached for the dog's tags on its collar.

"Bathsheba."

"What?" she asked, wiping the dog water off her face.

"That's what they named the dog. Nice people. They give their pet a biblical name, then leave him in the rain while they stay dry in a bar," I said.

"Hey, use this if you want to dry him off," Smitt said, offering a rag from under the front seat.

Maray grabbed it and began rubbing Bathsheba down. He was apparently very appreciative, because he jumped in her face and tried to lick her.

It was amazing to see Maray happy and laughing. Maybe she needed a dog...

Bathsheba, now warm and dry, made himself at home on the seat between Maray and myself, with his head on her thigh.

I had to admit. I was a tiny bit jealous.

"What are you doing?" Maray asked as I scrolled through my phone.

"Looking for a dog-friendly café. I thought it might be nice to get something warm to drink." I leaned down toward the dog. "What do you think, Bathsheba?" I pulled back just in time for his attempt to lick my face. He got me anyway, stinky breath and all.

19

LEO

THE DOG SNUGGLED into Maray's lap as she sipped her mint tea, leaning back comfortably on one of those broken-down couches coffee shops always seemed to have.

I took a drag on my black coffee and set it on the newspaper-scattered table before us.

"What are we gonna do with our new little friend?" Maray asked, pressing her nose against his.

Little fellow was in love with her. It was easy to see why.

"We're going to give him back."

Her face fell for a moment, then bounced back. "You're right. We can't keep him. We gotta return him. But the owner will have learned a lesson."

Bathsheba stepped from Maray's lap and snuggled

into mine. Christ, I was kind of falling for him, too. I couldn't fucking believe someone would leave their dog tied up in the rain.

"Maray, I wanted to talk to you again about working for the club. I know you need work, and this offer is pretty lucrative. It could relieve a lot of your financial pressures."

She looked up from the dog and bit her lip. "It does sound… interesting. What would I be doing?"

I could think of a few things I'd like her to do…

"You'd be keeping track of the games—who won and lost—that sort of thing. Since we don't deal in cash, we need to wire money to the winners, and charge the losers. It's pretty easy stuff. We just need people we can trust."

She smiled at me and tilted her head. "You trust me, Leo?"

Holy fuck. She was actually flirting with me.

I just looked at her, taking in her ringed blue eyes, full lips, and flawless skin. She was so perfect she almost looked like a doll. And she had no idea.

"Yeah. I trust you." I reached for her hand. "You trust *me*?"

She gripped my fingers back. Good sign.

"I don't know. I mean, you are kind of a thug."

I had to smile at that. In fact, I dropped my head back and laughed so hard everyone in the café turned to look at me.

"What's so funny?"

I actually had to wipe tears from my eyes. "You said *thug*. It's such a quaint term. I love it. You crack me up, Maray Stone."

Petting Bathsheba, she smiled at me.

"Here. Put this cover on your tea," I said, handing her a lid. "We're going shopping."

She frowned. "Why? For what?"

"You need some new clothes if you're going to work at the club."

We pushed through the revolving doors at Saks, the literal scene of the crime, with Bathsheba in Maray's arms. I doubted the store loved the idea of shoppers bringing their pets along, but as long as the dog stayed mellow, I knew they'd leave us alone.

Especially when they realized how much money I'd be spending.

Maray walked stiffly alongside me, clearly nervous about returning to the store.

I leaned close to her. "Relax. I'm not turning you in, okay?"

She looked at me, trying to hide her grim expression. "It's just… uncomfortable. But I'll be okay."

She forced a tight little smile.

We got on the elevator and pressed the button for the women's floor. The doors opened, and we maneuvered to get out—such was shopping with New York City crowds.

Maray clutched Bathsheba closer to her chest and looked at the expensive women's clothing like a fish out of water.

"Hey, relax. You belong here just as much as anyone. Half the people who shop here afford to do it only because they have credit card debt out the ass."

She shrugged. "I've only ever been on the first floor. You know, where we… um, met. It's so beautiful here. And the salesladies are so elegant."

I turned her to face me. "Do not feel intimidated by anything about this place. You are a smart, accomplished woman. Take pride in that."

Surprise washed over her face and her eyes watered for an instant. "Thank you," she said quietly.

She sniffled and cleared her throat.

So, I took her hand.

"May I help you today?" an impossibly tall, thin woman asked, greeting us with a warm smile.

She moved to tickle the dog under his chin, and Maray's hand relaxed a little in mine.

"Yes, thank you. Say, I was wondering if you could call my personal shopper, Frank, for me. I texted him that we'd be by. The name is Leo Borroni."

She nodded and gestured for us to follow her.

"You have a personal shopper?" she asked.

I shrugged, leaning close to her. Christ I was dying to kiss her. "Yup."

She raised her eyebrows and followed the saleslady into a sumptuous dressing room with expensive artwork and furniture, a giant mirror with a small platform in front of it for standing on, and a bar cart holding chilling champagne.

Where was my scotch? Frank always hooked me up.

"Heyyyyy!" Frank crooned, flying into the room. He turned to the saleslady, who stood in the doorway, smiling. "We're good now, Lilla. Thanks."

He pulled the door shut right in her face. Frank was serious about his sales. No doubt about it.

He ran over to Maray. "Look at you," he said breathily, turning her and stepping back to admire her.

"Leo, this woman has the face of a fucking angel," he said, shaking his head. I could swear he wiped away a tear. He placed his hands on either side of her face and kissed her forehead.

"Just had to do that. Hope you don't mind." He grabbed Maray's hand and pulled her over to the sofa, where he sat, still holding her hand like they were best friends.

Bathsheba reached out and licked Frank's face, which caused him to shriek.

"No, no, little doggy. Do not be licking me. Daddy just had a very expensive facial."

He tore his gaze away from Maray, and looked at me. "Leo. How're you doing, honey?" Suddenly, his hands flew to his face. "Fuck. I forgot your scotch."

Running to the dressing room door, he yanked it open and screamed, "Lilla!"

She appeared so fast I wondered if she'd been waiting outside the door.

"Go upstairs to Men's and get the scotch." Then he slammed the door again in her face.

He sat back down and stared at Maray for a moment. "Okay, baby. Let's talk about your style. And give Leo the dog. I don't want his hair all over our clothes."

Maray passed me Bathsheba. "I... I'm not sure of my style. I mean, I'm in college, so I'm pretty casual. You know, jeans, sneakers, boots. Although, I do have a formal coming up, for my sorority."

Frank wrinkled his nose. "Oh, you're in a *sorority*. Gotcha. Well, we'll make sure you look better than any of those other girls. I know how y'all are competitive."

Maray's face brightened, clearly pleased to have Frank on her side.

"I'd like to see her in a variety of things," I said. "You know, some nice pants and blouses. Evening stuff, too."

He put his hands on his hips and stared me down. "Leo, I know just how you'd like to see this beauty dressed. I also know you'd like to see her *undressed*, too. Amiright?"

He tossed back his head, laughing.

20

MARAY

HOLY CRAP. I was in a super-fancy dressing room trying on super-expensive clothes, all chosen by a super-gay personal shopper.

I was in heaven.

Who knew you got a private dressing room in these fancy stores? It reminded me of the salon-y type of waiting room I hung out in ages ago when one of my cousins was trying on wedding dresses.

I was supposed to be in her wedding, so she'd dragged all the bridesmaids and me to one of the most expensive bridal salons in town. I sat for hours eating candy-coated almonds, and dutifully ooh'ed and aah'ed when all the other girls did. I even managed to shed a tear at one frilly, ugly confection she'd fallen in love with.

Then it was time to focus on bridesmaids' dresses. She wanted everyone to try on the same dress to make sure we looked perfect in it. One by one, we did, because those salons only have one sample of each dress. When my turn came, I couldn't get it over my big booty. To be fair to myself, the samples were like size six, and the other girls trying them on had been starving themselves for weeks in preparation for the day. So my size ten bum was in proportion to the rest of me. Yeah, at a size ten, I was the *fat* girl in the wedding.

But today was nothing like that. I felt like a million bucks, and all the clothes looked amazing on my booty. Frank brought me beautiful outfit after beautiful outfit —wide-legged palazzo pants, silky low-cut blouses, a couple wrap dresses, and of course, something special for my formal.

He had some sort of magic ability to look at me and know what would work on my body. I just hoped he didn't know I'd stolen a very expensive item from the very store where we were only a week earlier.

"Okay. All zipped up. Now, what do you think?" He turned me toward the mirror and stepped back, a finger tapping his chin as he looked me up and down. "Yes. *This.*"

I hardly recognized myself in the mirror. He'd dressed me in a blue sequin number with what I think you call a 'fishtail' train. This gave the dress enough curve to make my waist look tiny, and my booty look—

well, like the good-sized booty it was. And as an added bonus, its built-in corset pushed the girls up to maximum exposure.

He was right.

It *worked*.

I couldn't wait to see the other girls drool.

"All right, princess. Go show Leo. Hopefully he won't tear it off you right here in the store and have his way with you." He slapped his thigh and cackled.

I didn't have the heart to tell him it wasn't like that between Leo and me. Yeah, he was gorgeous and all, and if I wasn't mistaken there was a bit of attraction going on between us. But I was no more the kind of woman he dated than he was the kind of guy I was interested in. No, we weren't meant to be.

But when Leo saw me in my blue dress, I began to wonder otherwise.

He glanced up from the magazine he'd been leafing through with Bathsheba sleeping in his lap. Leo's lips, usually drawn into a slightly lopsided smirk, parted slightly. Without a sound, he scanned me head to toe, and then his gaze went directly to mine.

Instead of staring at my tits and ass, he was looking at *me*. Really looking.

In the background, Frank giggled and left us, closing the door behind himself.

Leo set the dog down and without breaking our gaze, slowly walked toward me. I was nearly his height with the skyscraper Louboutins I was wearing. He took a loose strand of hair that had fallen out of the messy bun I'd tied, and ran it through his fingers to the ends.

I'd be lying if I didn't say I was scared to death. I mean, I wasn't the kind of woman he hung out with. What was he doing, looking at me like that?

With my hair between his fingers, he tugged. Hard.

My head snapped back, and I let out the tiniest moan. I hadn't meant to—it was reflexive. Kind of like the throbbing between my legs.

And from the awkward way my head was bent, I saw his eyes get darker than their usual dark brown.

How was that even possible?

He wove his fingers through the rest of my hair, knocking my loose bun right out of its knot. He pulled my face so close I could feel his breath and smell the scotch he'd been sipping.

We remained that way, exquisitely and painfully aware of each other. I wanted to kiss him. But I also wanted him to make the first move.

C'mon, Leo. Don't let a girl down.

In my heels, under the hot dressing room lights, and with my head pulled back at a strange angle, a woozy sensation washed over me. I closed my eyes as fuzziness filled my brain and a trickle of perspiration ran down my lower back.

Then everything went black.

"Here, sweetie, drink this."

Holy crap. I was laid out on the dressing room sofa with my head in Leo's lap, and Frank hovering over us trying to get me to drink water.

I pushed myself up, but a wave of dizziness whacked me, pushing me right back down.

"What happened?" I murmured. I was still in the sequined dress, but my shoes had been removed.

Leo ran his hand down my cheek, and my eyes fluttered closed. "You fainted."

"You ready to sit up, darlin'?" Frank asked.

I forced my eyes open and nodded. Taking a deep breath, I rose with Leo's help. Swinging my legs off the sofa, I shook my head to clear the cobwebs and found Bathsheba whining and running back and forth in front of me.

"Wow. That was weird." I took the water bottle from Frank and took a big gulp, then leaned to tickle the dog under his chin.

"Easy, cowgirl," Leo said, taking the bottle from me. "Small sips."

Frank stood in front of me. "Let's see if we can get you to stand. I think you'll feel a lot better when we get this tight dress off you."

He grasped my hands and hoisted me to standing.

Another wave of fuzziness washed over me, but this time it wasn't as strong and I shook it off.

"C'mon, girlfriend, let's get you changed," Frank

said, walking me behind the dressing room's curtain. "I can't have you puking on that thing."

As soon as the dress was off, I plopped down on a chair and Frank handed me my clothes to put back on. He'd told me not to feel shy about undressing in front of him. He saw naked men and women all day long, he'd assured me, probably more than most doctors did.

I didn't doubt it.

He bent near me and lowered his voice. "Leo said to pack everything up. *Everything.* Girl, you're walking out of here with a whole new wardrobe."

Shit. What would I do with all my fancy new clothes? And more importantly, could I keep my sorority sisters away from them?

"You know, Maray," Frank continued, "I've never seen Leo come in here with any other woman. How long have you two been going out?"

I watched him expertly fold several cashmere sweaters and place the rest of the clothes in hanging garment bags.

"Um, well, we're not," I answered.

He smiled and patted my cheek. "Well if you're not a couple yet, you soon will be."

He laughed at the shock on my face.

"Look, sweetie. I meet a lot of people. I know a few things."

And I, apparently, knew nothing.

"He's got it bad for you."

21

MARAY

SMITT DROVE us back across town to my dorm, with Bathsheba in my lap and the car trunk laden with my new things. What the hell was I going to do with it all?

"Leo, you were really too generous. I'm not sure I need all these things. Seriously."

Maybe I could return some of them. He'd never know. Right?

"Accept them as a gift. You'll need them for your job at the club."

I wasn't going to win this one.

"Hey, Leo?" I asked, summoning my courage.

"Yes, Maray?" He tilted his head and reached across the seat to clasp my fingers.

Okay. Something was definitely up. Maybe there'd been some truth to what Frank had said.

"If memory serves, just before I passed out, it seemed like you were going to kiss me."

God, don't humiliate me. Please.

"Really? Is that what you remember?" he asked.

I shook my head. "I don't know. Wouldn't that be funny? You and me kissing."

Had it all just been my imagination?

I snatched my hand back and looked out the car window. The car I'd been spending an *awful* lot of time in.

"Here ya go, Maray," Smitt called over his shoulder, pulling up in front of my dorm. "Want me to help carry all your loot in?"

My moment with Leo was over. Whatever. It was for the best.

I passed Bathsheba to him before he could say anything and jumped out of the car.

"Thanks for the shopping spree," I called through the open window.

Leo looked like he was going to say something but didn't. His lips just returned to that gorgeous half-smirk he wore all the time.

I skipped up the steps to my building with Smitt on my tail, holding the bulk of the garment bags Frank had packed up for me.

My next challenge was getting them into my room without attracting too much attention.

I turned to Smitt in the elevator. "We're gonna just blast through the hallway straight to my room. I don't want to get stuck talking to anyone and have them start asking questions."

"Aye aye, sailor," Smitt said with a nod.

"So how long have you worked for Leo?" I asked as we neared my floor.

He tilted his head like he was counting the years. "Long time, Maray. A long time."

Okay. I wasn't going to get much of anything out of him, it seemed.

The elevator opened. From where I stood, I could see a couple doors sitting wide open, and light music played somewhere. We hustled down the hall, and when we reached my room, I directed Smitt to just drop everything on my bed.

"Thanks, Smitt. See ya later."

He saluted me with a smile and took off.

I closed my bedroom door and locked it so no one could wander in unannounced. Then I went back to the garment bags. Shit. What was I going to do with everything?

I opened one and fingered of a pair of wool crepe evening pants. Before today, I'd never even known there was such a thing as 'evening pants.' Clearly if I were to become a fixture in Leo's world, I had a thing or two to learn.

What a minute.

We were not a couple, nor would we ever be.

He had fake-kissed me just to mess with me, my fainting episode giving him the upper hand.

Dammit.

He was probably gloating in the back of his Town Car right now, thinking I had the hots for *him*.

Well, he had another thing coming.

I started cleaning out space in the back of my closet as I thought through my 'tasks.' First the newspapers, then the wallet, and now the dog. What would be next?

Would there even be a next?

I hoped not.

I really did.

Okay, I didn't. I mean, I wanted to see the bastard again. I couldn't deny it.

Shit.

It was funny, the tasks he'd chosen for me. The newspaper guy and the dog owner were both jerks who needed to be taught a lesson. I couldn't deny it felt kind of good to put them in their place. I felt so self-righteous, like I'd done the world a favor, rather than committed an actual crime. And the opportunity to get Bathsheba out of the rain was downright magical.

But not so fast. I had my own transgression to face.

Was that part of Leo's plan for me? By putting others in their place, was he putting me in mine, as well?

The bottom line was, the man was a manipulative ass. And he was fucking with me. No doubt about it. And the more I thought about it, the more pissed I got. The daily humiliations I suffered at the hands of my sorority sisters weren't enough. Now I had to deal with some weirdo I'd met in a department store, who was really sticking it to me.

Just when I'd stuffed the last of my new clothes in the back of my closet, a key turned in my bedroom door.

"Damn, girl," Vivian hollered, throwing her arms around me. "I feel like I never see you anymore."

"What? I'm around. Just super busy," I said, scanning to make sure I'd hidden all the evidence.

She plopped down on her bed. "Yeah? How's Bagelry?"

Guess she hadn't noticed their quick demise.

"Um, they closed, Viv. Packed up shop and split."

Her mouth dropped open. "Are you shitting me? That place was a gold mine. Too bad. You getting a new job?"

Crap. I'd left one Saks shopping bag on my bed. I quickly sat down in front of it.

"Yeah, I need to. Anyway, the Bagelry owner was a prick. So I guess what goes around, comes around."

She threw her boots off and lay back on her bed, studying her fingernails. "Yeah. Guess so. Hey, you want to go to the library and study tonight?"

With Vivian focused on her manicure, I pulled my bedcovers over the shopping bag. Close call.

"Sure. Let's do that," I said.

Just as I'd hidden the bag, Vivian bolted upright. "Hey. Some of the other girls said they'd seen you hanging out with an older guy. A very good-looking older guy."

I shrugged it off. "It's nothing. Just someone I met when we went out a couple weeks ago."

A sly smile spread across her face. "Apparently you were in his *Town Car*? And he had a *driver*?"

I avoided her gaze by rummaging through my backpack for my ringing cell phone. "Yeah."

She *huffed* loudly. "Okay. You don't want to talk about it. I'll drop it." She pulled her boots back on.

Thank god.

"But I gotta tell you, Mar, it sounds like you have a sugar daddy."

"Hello?" I said, when I'd swiped my phone open.

"Hey, beautiful."

Leo's voice hit me like an electrical shock, even if he had been a jerk by not kissing me just an hour earlier.

"Oh hi, Leo."

I held a finger up to Vivian and pointed at the phone. She rolled her eyes and stood with her hands on her hips.

"I'm heading over to the library to study with my roommate."

Vivian tapped her foot.

"Tell her to go on without you."

"Um, why? I mean, I can't. I need to study."

"Your studies will be fine. Get dressed in some of your new clothes. I'll pick you up in twenty minutes. We're going to dinner."

And he was gone.

"Don't tell me. You're blowing off studying for your rich man-toy?"

I reached for Vivian's arm. "I'm sorry. He really wants to see me to… talk about something."

She cocked her head. "You won't tell me a thing about the guy, and yet he calls you for a last-minute booty call and you jump. You'd better fill me in on what you have going on, girlfriend."

"Okay. Okay, I will. Tomorrow, I'll tell you everything. But listen, it's not a booty call. It's not like that."

I didn't know what I was going to tell her, but at least I'd have time to think about crafting a believable story.

"Whatever," she said and sauntered down the hall toward the elevator. I watched her go, and just before the doors opened, she turned back to me and winked.

"Have fun tonight."

22

MARAY

IN A LIGHT DRIZZLE OF RAIN, Leo and I ran from the car to the restaurant.

"Are you wet?" he asked, sliding my new trench coat off my shoulders and handing it to the coat check.

"A little," I chirped.

Yeah, I'd gotten wet. Now my hair was going to frizz. I was fidgeting with it when Leo turned back from the coat check.

He froze in place, giving me the same look he had in the dressing room earlier that day.

Only this time, I wasn't giving him the chance to get close to me—and I certainly wasn't going to faint. I ignored him and followed the maitre'd to our table.

Thanks to the time I'd spent with the personal shopper, I knew exactly what outfit to put together and how. I'd chosen a form fitting pencil skirt and sleeve-less silk blouse with a ruffle down the front. I was wearing a red pair of Louboutins and thigh-high stockings—not that Leo could see that last bit.

He wasn't going to see them, either. I wore them to feel sexy. And they were working.

I hadn't had much time to get ready, but the good old internet was there to help. I found a video on doing a 'smoky eye,' and I had to say I pulled it off pretty well, finishing my look with a neutral lipstick. I teased my hair a little at the crown, and was good to go.

As soon as we were settled into our table, Leo reached for my arm. However, I pulled back with a breezy laugh. "I'm starving. What shall we have?" I said as I poured over the menu.

The smirk on his face grew. He knew what I was up to. Game on.

After a minute had passed, he tried again. Leaning over the table toward me, he said, "You're beautiful, you know."

Well. He was working harder than I thought he would. I mean, a guy like him? He could have any girl he wanted. Probably just snapped his fingers and the panties flew off everywhere he went.

"Thanks," I said, without looking up from my menu. "Hey, what are we doing about Bathsheba?"

"Returning him eventually. Maray, look at me."

I ran my finger down the list of fancy drinks. "Oh,

look. They have a drink with gin called the Bombshelter. I'll try that."

I finally looked up at him, my eyebrows raised. "Yes?"

"I mean it," he said.

I looked around the restaurant casually, as if I were checking out the décor. "Mean what?" I said, after a moment.

"You're fucking beautiful. Do you know that?"

This time he'd caught my gaze, and there was no looking away, damn him. How did he do that?

And in an instant, my surly attitude melted away. Without thinking about it, my hand reached across the table for his.

Oh my god. What was I doing?

I swear he would have held my hand the entire dinner if it had been possible. He barely took his eyes off me as we chatted about everything and nothing through possibly the most divine meal I'd had in my entire lifetime.

The only distraction was a loudmouth two tables over, alternating between bragging to his dinner companion and scrolling through his phone.

As we indulged in dessert, Leo glanced at the man, then back to me.

Uh-oh.

"What? What do I have to do?" I asked, even though I knew.

"The woman he's with just went to the restroom. I'll say hi to him, and you grab his phone."

Oh god.

Leo approached the man from an angle that forced him to turn away from his table and quietly asked him if they hadn't gone to college together. The man was somewhat annoyed by the interruption, but he set down his phone to stand up and shake hands when Leo offered his.

I wandered past as if I were searching for the ladies' room and grabbed the phone.

Done. I continued for the front door, slipping it into my bag.

Leo met me at the front, held my coat as I slipped into it, and we walked out.

The man was going to flip when he realized his phone was gone. There was something funny and so massively satisfying about sticking it to a jerk. I needed to do things like this more often.

I started to laugh.

I couldn't stop. Then Leo joined me.

The sky opened up and it began to pour. Smitt and the car were nowhere in sight, so we ran around the corner to an alley with a flimsy, leaking overhang, protecting us from the worst of the deluge but hardly keeping us dry. The rain slammed on the ground around us, splashing my legs and brand new shoes. But I didn't care.

Because Leo finally kissed me.

23

LEO

WHEN I PULLED Maray into the alley, it wasn't to escape the rain. No, we could have done that by running back in the restaurant.

I wasn't so much worried about the rain as I was how Maray would react to an overture of mine in public. I usually read a woman's signals without any trouble, and hell—who was I kidding?—I couldn't remember a time when I'd been turned down. But this woman was different. And that's what I liked about her.

Once in the alley and shrouded in semi-privacy, I backed her against a wet brick wall. With my hand under her chin, I pressed into her, our lips so close I could feel her breath. Her eyes stayed open, our gazes locked, until I tilted my head and pressed my lips to hers.

She was soft and pliant, as I knew she'd be, and she tasted of the expensive red wine she'd had with her meal. A soft moan vibrated in her throat, and she arched into me, undoubtedly aware of my hard cock.

I kissed her harder, knowing her lips would be swollen and sore later.

She needed something to remember me by.

Her hands threaded through my own hair, and she pulled me closer as her lips parted in invitation.

I couldn't lie. It was like the world around us had stopped. I could no longer see, hear, or feel the rain. All I knew was that I wanted to devour this woman.

But I also knew I had to take my time.

I stepped back and ran my lips down her neck. She gasped when my fingers trickled over her breast and closed in on her nipple through her silk blouse.

"Leo," she murmured.

I pulled back to look at her half-lidded eyes and wet lips. She was so fucking angelic, it was impossible to look away. I pulled her hand to my lips and held it there for a moment.

But we couldn't stay in that alley all night. We had things to do yet, and besides, I planned to take things one step at a time with my girl.

Shit. Did I really just say *my girl*?

We bolted from the alley to stand under the restaurant awning, where the guy whose phone we'd stolen was yelling at the poor teenage valet.

"I'm sorry, sir, but you'll have to talk to the manager about your missing phone. I just park the cars here," he pleaded, trying to hand the asshole the keys to his BMW 8 Series and get rid of him.

The now-phoneless loudmouth took a deep breath and rolled his eyes. "Okay, fine. Get the goddamn manager."

The kid looked relieved to be able to pass an irate customer off to someone with more authority. "Please come with me," he said, holding open the restaurant door for them to go back in.

Some unlucky bastard was about to get his ass chewed out.

The guy's date, who'd been standing a few feet behind him, ran after them.

Maray's eyes were wide. "Wow. And to think I have his phone right here in my bag. Good thing it didn't ring."

She checked in her purse as if to make sure it was still there, then looked around. "Where's Smitt?"

"We don't need him," I said, stepping behind the stand that was the valet station.

Sitting on top of it were the angry guy's BMW keys. In his near panic, the valet had left them there.

I pressed the unlock button, and the car in front of us beeped.

"We have another way to get around," I told her, taking her hand.

"Huh? What do you mean? And what are you doing with those keys?"

I pulled the driver's-side door open. "You're right. They don't belong to us. We're just going to borrow them."

She looked from me, to the car, and back, confusion crossing her face. Then, her eyes widened.

"No way," she breathed.

"C'mon. Get in. You're driving," I said, holding the door open for her. "Hurry up, before they return."

"Oh my god," she said, running as best she could in her heels.

I handed her the keys, and she jumped in. I pushed her door closed and bolted over to the passenger side. The minute I was in, Maray had the car in drive, and we disappeared down the street.

"Oh my god, oh my god, oh my god. I just stole a fucking car."

"We're just *borrowing* it," I clarified.

I looked around the inside of the BMW. Of course the douche had the top-of-the-line model. He needed to impress his dates somehow, since his personality wasn't going to cut it.

"Ever drive a car like this?" I asked as she squealed around a corner.

She shook her head, rain-wet hair sticking to her

face. "No. It's fun," she laughed, taking another corner a bit too fast.

"Go up Third. The lights are timed."

She glanced at me. "Okay."

When we got to Third, there was a wave of green traffic lights before us.

"Okay. Now open her up."

She took a deep breath and pressed the gas. The eight-cylinder engine shot up the street, leaving every other vehicle in its dust, until we landed in the far reaches of Manhattan.

"Holy shit, this thing is fast. How long are we going to keep it?"

"How long do you think we should?"

She pulled the car over, under one of the bridges that crossed the East River. Which one, I wasn't sure. I'd not been able to take my eyes off her.

God, what a pussy I was.

She put the car in park and turning in the driver seat, reached for my hands. Hers looked so small in mine as she stroked my palm, humming lightly. Christ, what this woman did to me. It should have been illegal.

Like all the other things we'd been doing.

She cupped my face, and we leaned toward each other for a slow, exploring kiss.

I reached behind her, grabbing a fistful of hair, and her breath quickened. "You're not only beautiful Maray, you're also sexy as fuck."

She smiled and tilted her head. "Thank you."

I texted Smitt to come pick us up, and we kissed some more.

"How about I put the phone in the glove box? We can leave the keys on the back tire," she suggested.

I beamed. I couldn't help it. My girl was learning.

Just as we settled ourselves into the Town Car Smitt was driving, two police cars came screaming into the empty lot where we'd abandoned the BMW.

"Oh my god! We're busted!" Maray cried, craning her neck to see what was going on.

I put my hand on her arm. "Relax, baby. Everything will be fine."

She looked around in a panic, as if for an escape. But there was none. Just like when I'd nabbed her shoplifting.

The cop car pulled up alongside us, and both Smitt and I rolled down our windows.

"Our fingerprints are all over that car," she whispered. "Oh my god, we're fucked."

I squeezed her hand to snap her out of her panic. "Calm down," I told her quietly.

The cop closest to us shined his flashlight into our car and moved it around to check us out, studying each one of us individually. We were all squinting and could barely see him behind the light.

"What are you folks doing here?" he demanded.

Smitt cleared his throat. "I'm their driver, sir. I, um, brought them here so they could have some private time. I was about to get out for a smoke while they, uh, you know, talked."

Holy shit, he was good. I was going to have to give him a nice little bonus for his fast thinking.

The flashlight shined in the back seat, illuminating Maray and me for a second time.

"Good evening, officer," I said with a nod.

"Uh-huh," he mumbled.

He looked past our car at the BMW we'd gotten out of only moments earlier. Our timing, and Smitt's, had been beyond perfect.

"We got a report about a stolen car, tracked via GPS. Did you see anyone get in or out of that BMW over there?" the cop asked, gesturing with his bright light.

We all turned to take a look and shook our heads.

"No sir, it was here when we arrived. Haven't seen anyone," Smitt lied. "I was kind of wondering what it was doing there. Figured it must have been stolen."

Must have?

"Well, okay. Folks, you need to be on your way. You shouldn't hang out in vacant lots like this. You don't know what kind of trouble you'll get into. They're not safe."

"Will do, Officer. Thank you." Smitt rolled up all the car windows and slowly drove out of the bumpy parking lot and back onto the city streets.

Even in the dark, Maray's face registered pure shock.

"You handled yourself perfectly, Maray," I said. "Good job to you, too, Smitt."

He nodded from the front seat.

Maray just kept looking ahead. "I… I… I could have been arrested."

Was that just now dawning on her?

"Well, you weren't, and the asshole from the restaurant will be getting his phone and car back in perfect condition."

She took a deep breath, and slowly released it. "I was kind of freaking back there."

"I noticed."

She looked over at me. "It *was* kind of fun though, I have to admit."

I pressed a button on my armrest, and a dark black window rose between the front and back seats.

"How'd you do that?" Maray asked, looking around.

"Magic. Figured we could use some privacy."

A smile crept over her face. "Privacy? Why do we need that?"

God she was hot when she was being coy.

I pulled her closer and ran a finger down one side of her face and across her lips, which trembled at my touch. I ran it back and forth, then worked it into her mouth, which parted just enough to allow me in. Her mouth pursed like a kiss and she sucked me, her eyes fluttering closed.

I reached a hand under her ass and gripped her curvy flesh, squeezing until she sucked my finger harder. It was all I could do not to explode, because I kept imagining putting my hard cock where my finger was.

But there'd be time for that later.

I slid another finger in her mouth and reached under her skirt.

Dayum. She was wearing stockings. Thigh-highs, at that. My worst kind of kryptonite.

Slow down, boy.

"Nice," I murmured, smoothing my hand over the silky fabric up to her warm thigh. I reached a little further and found the lace of her thong panty, which I began to ease down under her ass.

She continued sucking me like a champ, all while my dick was ready to burst out of my goddamn trousers.

I got her thong down to her ankles, and pulling one foot out, I pushed her knees as far open as her narrow skirt would permit. My fingers slipped back underneath, dancing along her inner thighs, easing closer and closer to her sex. When I finally reached her shaved cleft, I ran a finger through her wet slit. Pushing between her pussy lips just enough to reach her clit, I found the hard little nub that I planned to get my mouth on at some point.

With my other hand, I pushed my fingers into her mouth to the point where her eyes watered and little black smudges of makeup pooled under them. I made circles on her clit at the same time, soft and slow at first, then faster and harder, until she moaned through her full mouth.

She bucked against my strokes, pulling her skirt above her ass to spread her legs further. Opening her legs, she arched her back to give me perfect access.

Between the motion of the car, and the rhythm of my hand, she started shaking. I pulled my fingers from her mouth, and she gasped at the abrupt emptiness. She lifted her head and her gaze locked with mine, and I could swear I'd never seen anything like it.

"Come for me, baby. Come on my hand," I demanded

In moments, her head fell to her chest. "Oh god... Leo, I'm coming," she murmured so quietly I hardly heard her.

But I certainly felt her shuddering as she bucked against my hand.

I licked my fingers and she was sweet like I knew she'd be. It was just a matter of time before I'd have my face between her legs for more.

She eased her skirt down to her knees in an effort to put herself back together. She straightened her blouse and hair and put her damp shoes back on, which had come off in all the commotion.

"What a night," I muttered.

She leaned her head on my shoulder and yawned, snuggling into me. "Thank you."

I opened the glass separating us from the front seat. "Smitt, let's take Maray back to her dorm before she falls asleep."

Yeah, I wanted her to spend the night with me, but the time wasn't right.

It would be, though, soon.

24

MARAY

Leo shook me gently.

We pulled up in front of my dorm, thank goodness, because I'd dozed off. But, I wanted to get one thing out in the air before the evening was over.

Before the *incredible* evening was over.

"So, when can I quit?" I asked.

It was dark in the car, but the streetlights illuminated Leo's handsome face just enough to reveal the question mark on his face. "Quit? Quit what?" he asked.

"The tasks. You know. This stealing stuff. My penance for—" I lowered my voice, although I had no idea why, "—taking that bag from Saks."

Yeah, I was ashamed. Guess I always would be.

He looked at me, thinking. "Right. Well, you're nearly done."

I supposed that was good news. But weren't four tasks enough?

"I have to take it up with the guys. You know, since we all took bets… on you."

I could swear something like regret passed over his face. It was kind of heartwarming, that he might feel a little shitty for exploiting me and my bad choices. So I dropped it.

"Okay," I said. "Don't forget, we need to return Bathsheba."

He nodded. "The girls at the club are going to miss him. It's kind of a shame. He's a sweet little guy."

"Why don't you get your own dog? He could be the mascot of the club. Call him 'Poker' or something like that."

Leo cracked up, something I'd never seen. It made him seem so… normal. "I'll tell you what. I will entertain the idea of getting a dog for the club if you come work for me."

Oh. Wow.

A dog *and* a bunch of money. Now he was talking.

"Mar! Haven't seen much of you lately. What's up with the formal?" Lulu asked, accosting me in the dorm hallway on my way out the next morning.

Shit. I hadn't thought about the formal in days. It was coming like a freight train.

"Oh, everything is great," I said breezily, continuing to walk.

Actually, everything *was* pretty much taken care of. All that was left was to stress out like a fool. Fortunately, with Leo up my ass and my new life of crime, I'd been too busy for any of that.

Crazy days. It certainly put silly sorority things into perspective.

"Are you *sure*?" she asked, squinting.

That question could not have come at a worse time. I was running late, a wreck about starting work at the club, and in a tizzy after my hot-as-hell make-out session with Leo in the back seat of his car.

I puffed up my chest, something I should have learned to do a long time ago. "You know, Lulu, if you don't like the way I'm doing things, then next time *you* can fucking run the show."

The look on her face was worth the price of admission. Her mouth opened, then snapped shut, her lips forming into a tight, thin line. She put her hands on her hips, and just when she was about to say something, the elevator opened.

"See ya," I hollered over my shoulder.

I was in no mood. I just wasn't.

I dropped my clothes from the rainy night before at the cleaner's on my way to class—fingers crossed they could make the soggy bundle look like new. I was normally loathe to spend on dry cleaning, but if Leo's predictions of my earnings at the club were anywhere close to accurate, I could afford to get my nice, new clothes properly cleaned and pressed.

I mean, he'd bought me all these nice things. Taking care of them was the least I could do.

As promised, Smitt pulled up in front of my dorm, where I was watching from my window, at exactly eight p.m. in the black Town Car where Leo and I had, um, been together the night before.

Oh my god had that been hot.

I hadn't been with many guys, so didn't have much to compare, but Leo's touch was like fire on my skin. He knew exactly when to go soft and when to go hard. Even a day later, my head was still spinning from it, and my sex was begging for more, like a starved little animal.

But did I want more? Could I *handle* more? My relationship with him was bizarre enough, as it was.

But dammit, I'd be lying if I didn't admit I lay in bed the night before imagining what he looked like naked, his head between my thighs, going to town on my girl parts. And I knew he'd be hot as shit without clothes on because you'd better believe I'd felt him up when we were messing around. There was not an ounce of fat on the man, and the ripples on his chest that I felt through his expensive cotton dress shirt were hard as rocks.

Seriously, though. What the hell was I doing? The man was extorting me to commit crimes—I would say petty, but stealing a car was not a petty crime, even if we did abandon it after a brief joyride. Additionally, he and his friends had made bets on me, he'd offered me a job at his sketchy card club with the promise of making a shit ton of money, and I couldn't stop fantasizing about his going down on me.

I was a freaking disaster. And I'd basically stolen from him, too, by hanging on to his money clip. What the hell was I going to do with that? How would I return it, now?

At the sight of the shiny Town Car, I took a deep breath and scooted out of my building, but not before taking one more look in the mirror and pulling my Burberry trench tight. I looked good. There was no denying it. I'd twisted my hair into a tight bun at the base of my neck, hoping to rock the sexy librarian look, and this time I'd lightened up on the smoky eye but had gone to town with an insanely bold lipstick I'd picked up at the drugstore. Either the upper half or the lower half of your face could sport dramatic makeup. If you did both, well, you looked like a drag queen.

I learned that from YouTube.

My hopes of sneaking out unnoticed were quickly dashed, however, like they nearly always were. I had no privacy—none. Well, unless I went to the bathroom, but half the time one of my sorority sisters insisted on talking to me in there, too.

Vivian was just returning from class when we collided in the doorway.

She looked me up and down with a low whistle.

"Damn. Someone's been shopping." She lowered her voice conspiratorially and smiled. "You *do* have a sugar daddy. You bad girl, you."

Only Vivian would think that was a good thing.

Inching away, I shook my head. "It's not like that. I got a new job and, um, they gave me a loan to get some nice clothes. You see, I have to get dressed up. I'm working at a club."

Her eyes widened at the sound of 'club.' It was a magic and powerful word in my world. "No shit. Oh my god, can you get me in? Which club is it?"

"Um, it's not your kind of club, Viv. It's one where dudes go to play poker."

Her face fell. "Oh. Shit. And here I thought you could get me on a VIP list."

I ran back and planted a kiss on her cheek. "You'll always be on *my* VIP list, Viv."

She rolled her eyes. "Oh god. Corny alert. Go. Get out of here."

What would Vivian think of Leo? I wasn't sure I wanted to know.

"Hey, Smitt, how are you tonight?" I asked, hopping in the Town Car's front seat.

With his hands on the wheel, he looked over at me. "You're welcome to sit in the back if you want. I don't mind. Driving people around is part of my job."

"I'll ride up here with you just this once, if you don't mind."

He shrugged and pulled into traffic.

"So, Smitt, how long did you say you'd been working with Leo?"

He leaned on the horn at a taxi driver who stopped right in front of us. "I didn't."

I wasn't giving up that easily.

"Okay. Then how long have you been with him?"

He was silent for a moment.

What was the big goddamn secret?

"Smitt. Should I not be asking you this stuff? Because if not, you can just tell me. Although I can't imagine why your approximate length of employment would be so top secret. I'm just making conversation," I huffed.

"I've been with the Borronis for a long, long time. Almost since we were kids."

"The Borronis? Like, plural. As in there are more than one?"

He nodded. "Yup. Leo and his twin brother, Luca. His identical twin brother. Back in Vegas."

Wait, wait, wait, wait, wait.

Leo had a freaking twin? There were *two* of them walking the face of this planet? How the hell did that happen?

The universe must have been on a perfection streak when it created those two.

How did I not know this? And what else did I not know about him?

"I guess I don't know Leo very well, now that I think about it," I said.

"He can be a hard guy to get to know. He's been through a lot. Doesn't open up easily. If ever," he said.

"Why is his brother in Vegas and he's here?" I asked as we pulled into the club's parking garage.

Damn. Out of time.

Smitt reached across me and opened my door so I could pop out. "*That* you'll have to ask him about."

Fine.

"Thanks for the ride, Smitt," I said. "You're not coming up?"

"I'll be up later. I'm picking up a couple of the players. Membership has its privileges."

He winked and was gone.

25

MARAY

As soon as I stepped off the elevator into the club, I nearly collided with a statuesque woman with short-cropped hair—the kind of hairstyle that worked on only certain people, but when it did, it was stunning. And it worked on her. I could hardly stop staring, thinking maybe I should try it.

Like I occasionally thought about cutting bangs.

Yeah, no.

She extended her hand. "I'm Delphine. Smitt let me know you were coming up."

"Nice to meet you," I said, shaking her hand. "Is Leo here, too?" I asked, looking around.

"He is," she said, smiling politely. "He's in his office, working. How about I show you what you'll be doing tonight?"

"Sure, thank you. I appreciate it. Where is Bathsheba?" I asked, following her.

She looked over her shoulder and gave me a beatific smile. "He's with Leo," she said simply.

Wow. I'd thought I'd be working side by side with the man. Dumb assumption. He had employees to run the club and his games. Like *me*.

"It may take a couple nights to come up to speed and feel completely comfortable with things, but don't worry. I'll help you," she said.

I hadn't known what to expect of the world of high-stakes poker, but I was pretty sure it wasn't going to be like Sunday night bingo. A bunch of dudes drinking and betting large sums of money? Sounded like the perfect ingredients for a testosterone-fueled shitshow. I was sure they had security measures out the yin-yang, but I could just imagine the tensions that simmered under the surface.

And what a relief that this woman was so nice to me, instead of being a shit like some of the girls at the sorority.

Jesus, if life wasn't one big huge *Survivor* episode.

She led the way to the game room where a table surrounded by chairs was smack in the middle. I'd passed by it on my way to the interrogation room only a couple days before. Little did I know then what was in store. From shoplifting to a new job in mere days.

Jesus.

Delphine explained the setup. "We adjust the size of

our tables depending on how many players we have coming on a given night. Tonight we have six players, so there's only one table out and it's sized accordingly. But we can add tables and actually have four different games going on at a time."

She took me to what looked like the head of the table. "I stand right here," she said, pointing.

"Why do you stand? Are you playing?"

A kind smile crossed her face. Shit, now she'd know how green I was.

"I'm the dealer, Maray."

"Right. Right," I said. As if I knew anything.

She pointed out the bar, where an even more beautiful woman organized glassware. "That's Samia. She'll serve drinks, food, that sort of thing. And you will sit over here." She beckoned me to follow.

I set my small purse underneath a counter-height table that would be my workplace for at least a few hours. All it held was a laptop and stacks of different colored chips.

"You will distribute the chips, keep track of who is buying and make sure they wire us the money for it, and record the players' wins and losses. You will be dealing with very large sums of money. We don't exchange cash here, so it's all wire transfers. Are you comfortable with that?"

My stomach acid churned, and I needed a drink of water. But I smiled bravely.

"Of course, Delphine. I'm a finance major, so this will be good experience."

She looked at me quizzically, failing to see the connection. But she continued, anyway, with the utmost courtesy. "Okay, then. I see the players are beginning to arrive. I have a couple more things to show you. If you have any questions, please ask. Oh, and Samia will be serving cocktails, if there is anything you'd like."

Really? I could drink on the job? Not that I wanted to, but I totally dug that I could.

While the arriving players greeted each other at the bar like old friends, Leo appeared, shaking hands and smacking them on the back with that bad-boy smirk he wore so well. He was dressed casually, without his usual necktie, but he still managed to look like a million beautiful bucks.

Funny thing was, he didn't look my way or even acknowledge me. It seemed strange, and more than a little annoying, but had anything else in my life been normal, lately? Maybe there was a *no fraternizing with the help* thing going on?

Who the hell knew what was normal in this world, but I tried to suppress the miffed feelings welling up in me anyway. I had no right to expect anything of this strange arrangement I'd fallen into. I was here to make some money, get out, and get back to my studies.

Delphine, who was still explaining the ins and outs of my new job, saw my gaze following Leo. She smiled slightly and kept talking about my responsibilities without missing a beat.

Her discretion was amazing, but I couldn't help but wonder if she'd seen my kind before? The hungry college girl, with puppy eyes for the big bad boss?

God, what a cliché I was.

Delphine walked me through the proprietary software program they used to keep track of everything.

Damn. They had a proprietary software program.

How much money flowed through the place, anyway?

"I'll be just over there at my station, Maray, but if you need anything, just wave me down."

The server, Samia, approached me, a stunning black beauty with natural hair.

"Hi there. Welcome aboard. Want a drink?"

My mouth was so dry I could hardly speak. "Thanks. I'd love some water. In fact, if you have a pitcher, that would be great. I have a feeling I'm going to be thirsty all night."

She laughed kindly. "Gotcha. Be right back."

Why wasn't I hanging with people like these women instead of my silly, vain sorority sisters?

Oh right, because sorority sisters would *help me get somewhere in life.*

Or so I'd been told.

After the players took their seats, Delphine helped me distribute chips to the players. It all seemed straightforward, and when she got to work dealing the game, I took a seat at my little table and dug around on the computer. Seemed there would be a lot of down-time in this job.

So, my thoughts wandered to Leo.

He'd disappeared after greeting the players. I was baffled that he'd not come over to say hello.

Maybe our sexy little trysts had been one-offs, which was fine, if that's how he wanted it. It wasn't like we'd discussed dating or being a couple.

Were my little 'tasks' over, too? It would be nice to know.

Over the next three hours, I handled my work like a pro. The players, in their casual clothes, looked like regular guys off the street. But when they got their chips and transferred funds in and out of accounts to the tune of tens of thousands of dollars, I knew I'd entered a strange universe.

"Hey, beautiful," a voice whispered in my ear, sending a startled shiver down my spine.

Well. He'd decided to say hi, after all, and apparently Bathsheba had followed him, because he started whining to be picked up. So, of course I did. I couldn't resist my little rescue.

With the dog nestled in my lap, I turned to find Leo inches from my ear, so close our noses nearly collided. The angles of his jawline were so finely sculptured it was all I could do to keep my fingers from stroking them. A surprise five-o'clock shadow grew on his normally clean-shaven face, and it was a devastatingly hot contrast to his perfectly pressed bespoke suit and dress shirt.

But it wasn't just his good looks that got my motor revving. There was something in his dark eyes that belied his thug persona. I could swear there was some sort of hurt deep down, and a level of sensitivity that he rarely, if ever, revealed.

Why was he showing this to me? Surely, he could have any woman he wanted, and there were a lot of women in New York far more exciting than broke, thieving college student *me*.

But my thoughts—and excitement at Leo's proximity—were interrupted by shouting coming from the direction of the card game.

A guy with curly red hair had jumped up from the table, causing his chair to topple back. His arms were flying emphatically, and he ran around the table like a madman, alternating between pulling his hair and clenching his fists like he wanted to hit someone. Behind him, I spotted the burly security guys closing in. Delphine backed away from the table, her darting eyes assessing the situation.

This had happened before. And they knew just what to do.

"Goddammit," he screamed, his voice breaking, "that was the last of my money, you fuckers." A sob escaped his throat, and he doubled over in tears. "I'm ruined," he screamed. "I'm ruined."

Christ, I'd thought they made sure these players had

enough money that they could afford to lose, before they were admitted as members. Seemed like there were some holes in Leo's system.

Nico and Colt appeared on the scene, and soon the man was surrounded by them and the guards.

"Tommy, calm down. Please calm down," Colt said quietly.

Tommy continued to sob, as the security guards took one arm each, and ushered him to another part of the club, presumably one where he could get his shit together.

Leo must have seen the horrified look on my face. "Hey," he said, walking over and putting a hand on my shoulder. "It happens sometimes. We try to weed out the folks who don't have the assets to play at this level, but sometimes people like Tommy get in and gamble everything they have, hoping for the big payout."

I took a gulp of water, my hands shaking. "Wow. I didn't know what he was going to do." Bathsheba, unfazed by the outburst, licked my face.

He looked around as Delphine took her place at the table again and continued the game. "That's why we have security. Emotions run high."

"Everyone knew exactly what to do. Guess this happens from time to time?" I asked.

"More often than we'd like. But we do have a protocol, as you saw. Nico and Colt play good cop, and if Dom and I need to step in, we play bad cop."

Okay, I didn't know what the hell that meant.

"Leo, I'm not sure this is for me."

The work was easy enough, and it was kind of fun to get all glammed up. But to watch a man ruin his life? No, thanks.

"I understand," he said quietly. "Now that you've tried it, if you don't like it, that's fine."

As my racing heart began to calm, I was thinking clearly again.

"It seems so dangerous, Leo. What if he'd had a gun when he freaked out?"

He shrugged. "The guys get patted down by security when they come in, and you saw how fast the guards worked. It happens. People get upset, they lose their shit. It's a difficult thing to see, but it's not really dangerous to anyone but the loser."

"I wonder how much he lost," I said, poking around in our software app for an answer.

Leo shook his head as his gaze drilled into mine.

"You don't want to know, baby. You do not want to know."

26

LEO

THAT NIGHT'S game broke up earlier than normal, spirits subdued by Tommy's meltdown. Yeah, people could lose their shirts in this business, it was a well-known fact, but everyone hated to see it nonetheless. Tommy had seemed like a nice guy, and no one wanted him to hit rock bottom like he had.

Especially not Maray.

She was clearly upset with what she'd witnessed. It was understandable. It's no fun realizing someone made a devastating mistake in gambling everything they had, and wondering if perhaps you played a small role in their undoing.

And Maray was particularly sensitive, which I appreciated. I was careful about who I chose for our

MIKA LANE

team, and I seriously hoped I could get her to stick around. She'd be great for the club.

And, of course, I'd get to see more of her. In fact, even if she wasn't great for the club, I'd still want her around.

Which scared me. I usually made sound business decisions.

Something was getting in the way, lately.

She was all decked out in one of the outfits I'd gotten her at Saks, and damn if she wasn't stunning. I mean, she was adorable in her college duds—jeans and sneakers—but she was pure elegance in her palazzo pants and silk blouse, wearing bright lipstick, with her hair all pulled back into a knot.

The players had noticed her, too, but they knew to stay away from my employees. Unless it was time to tip them on their way out.

I watched from the bar as each guy thanked her, handing her a palmful of folded-up bills. She smiled humbly and told them she looked forward to seeing them next time.

So, she was coming back. Cool. Of course, it was hard to say no to the kind of money she stood to earn.

Smitt showed everyone out, my partners having long since left to escort Tommy out of the building and home. Samia and Delphine said their good-nights, leaving the cleaning to the crew that would arrive in a few hours.

When Maray and I were alone, I could finally put

192

my arms around her. "Why don't you come home with me tonight?" I asked.

Surprise washed over her pretty face, which she quickly replaced with indifference.

"Oh, I don't know. I have to get up early to study."

Okay. Playing hard to get. It was cool. She'd probably learned it from her sorority sisters.

I ran my hand along her bare arm, starting at her shoulder, and down to her wrist. Then I took her hand and pulled it to my lips. I wanted to kiss her all over, but I'd start small.

"I have what you need for studying at my house. Come with me. You'll see," I said, putting her coat over her shoulders, grabbing Bathsheba, and leading her to the parking garage.

She followed without a word.

She'd not been to my place—hell, I brought very few women over, anyway—so when we walked into my spartan Midtown loft, her mouth dropped open. Bathsheba ran up the stairs, most likely to my bed, where he'd commandeered a sleeping spot for himself his first night there.

"I've never seen an apartment like this before," she breathed, doing a complete three-sixty. "I'm not sure whether I like it or not, but it's just so… different."

I had to laugh at her frankness.

"Yeah, it used to be a factory or something. When I moved here, I had it renovated into a living space but never did much about furnishing it. I know it's kind of cold," I said, following her gaze.

"Speaking of moving here, I didn't know you were from Las Vegas, or that you had a twin brother."

Christ. Someone had been doing some research.

"Well, it's not a secret. I guess we just haven't talked much about ourselves."

I caught her stifling a yawn.

"Let's go up to the loft. I'm tired, too."

Actually, I was exhausted.

I led her by the small office, just off the bedroom. "This is what I got for you, so you could study here if you want."

I'd outfitted the room with a new Mac and a copy of each of Maray's textbooks for the semester.

Her eyes widened as she looked from me to the books and back. "Oh my god. How did you know what books I was using?"

I placed my hands on either side of her face. "I know a lot of people. Remember?"

She put her hands on her hips. "Holy shit. You bought me a set of books. That was very generous. I mean, kind of weird, but generous."

"Yeah, well, I'm a weird guy."

"W… why did you do this? Create this set-up for me?" she asked.

I wasn't entirely sure I had an answer. But I could try. "I guess I hoped you'd want to spend some time here. With me."

Christ, I hadn't felt that way about anyone in a very long time, and it scared the shit out of me. Last time I had, it had not ended well.

We looked at each other for a long moment, without saying a word. Sometimes you didn't have to say anything to actually say a lot.

But I was getting uncomfortable. That was how I rolled. "C'mon, let's get some sleep."

With the dog at the end of the bed snoring lightly, Maray put on the long T-shirt I gave her and slipped under my down comforter. I crawled in behind her to spoon, kissed her, and fell asleep in moments.

Hours later, Bathsheba licked my face to let me know he needed to go out. I grunted and sat up, pulling on some sweats, when I realized Maray was no longer in my bed.

But there was keyboard clicking coming from the next room.

I peered around the corner into my office, and there sat Maray, wearing my bathrobe, books spread out on her desk, typing notes into her new computer. She glanced up at me from her work, smiled, and went back to her book.

I wasn't about to interrupt her, so I carried Bathsheba outside so he could take care of business and I thought about the day ahead.

I was ready—Maray was, too—for her to be done with her 'tasks.' But, my partners wanted to see our bet through to the end. They'd put up big money and wanted to see how it played out. So I calculated we needed one more undertaking before we could call it quits.

I couldn't believe how barely two weeks before I'd thought Maray was nothing more than a greedy college girl coveting something she couldn't afford, and I now knew her as a determined woman with principles and a big heart.

And sexiness to spare.

The way she responded to my touch, and the little noises she made when I brought her to orgasm, made my dick hard every time I thought about it. Yeah, there'd be more where that came from. Time was on our side.

Funny I was so taken by what my brother Luca would have called a girl 'from the straight side of the tracks.' We'd grown up surrounded by activities that weren't always on the up-and-up, thanks to our dad's mob connections, and that hadn't included a lot of people like Maray.

"You want coffee?" I asked her when I got back with the dog.

She smiled, so small in my huge robe, and held up a steaming mug. "I already helped myself. Hope you don't mind."

"Not at all. I'm going back to sleep." I walked over and kissed her temple.

She smiled at me and turned back to her books.

Shit. I was in trouble.

27

LEO

THE NEXT NIGHT, we had twenty players signed up, spread over three tables. We tried not to go over seven players per table on any given night—it made the game move too slowly. And of course, when we had multiple tables, we needed multiple dealers. But Delphine took care of all that.

The only remaining concern I had was whether Maray would be able to handle the work that came with such a crowd. It was one thing to be there with six players—twenty was a different story.

We'd returned Bathsheba to his owner earlier in the day. I was going to miss the little guy, I couldn't deny it.

I'd had Maray call the number on the dog's tags from one of our burner phones.

"Hello. Is this Bathsheba's owner?" she asked.

There was a lot of screaming coming from the earpiece of the phone.

"Hey, settle down," she said in a loud voice.

Damn, my girl was getting ballsy.

"Yeah, yeah. Whatever you say. Now, you will only get your dog back if you promise never to leave him out in the rain again."

I heard another string of hollering.

"Lady, if you're gonna be a bitch about it, I'll gladly keep the dog. He's quite happy with me, and I would never leave him in the rain."

The yelling subsided, replaced by a more moderate tone, presumably the woman making lame excuses.

"Great. Glad to hear it. I tell you what. I'll leave him outside the bar where I found him in the rain, when you were inside staying nice and dry. Remember that? But keep in mind, I'll be watching you. If I see Bathsheba mistreated in any way, you will lose him again. Permanently. And, I will inform animal control."

She rolled her eyes and shook her head. "I'm serious, lady. One screw-up and your dog-owning days will be over."

Maray closed the flip phone. "I kind of hate to say goodbye. He's such a good boy. And everyone at the club really likes him." She tried to stifle a sob.

Smitt turned onto the street where we'd found the dog.

"Want me to do it?" I offered.

She picked up the dog and kissed him. He eagerly

licked her back, blissfully unaware of the way we'd been negotiating for his well-being. "Yeah. You better do it. I'm not sure I can." Her chin shook, and she wiped at tears.

I let Bathsheba out of the car on his leash and quickly tied it to the bike rack where he'd been shivering in the rain. I jumped back in, and we watched for the owner.

A harried-looking woman came rushing around the corner minutes later and screamed when she saw her dog. She untied his leash, but he initially wouldn't go with her, barking and resisting. When she dropped to her knees and began to cry, he slowly walked up to her and licked her face. He jumped into her arms, and she smiled.

"Well, another day, another vigilante moment. I'm sorry to say goodbye to him, but he belongs with his owner." Maray looked out the window at the dog and owner as we pulled away from the curb.

"So I wanted to tell you, there is one more task," I said.

Her shoulders slumped. "Are you serious? Oh my god. What is it?" she asked, rolling her eyes.

"I don't know yet. But I do know I'm glad you're helping out tonight. It's gonna be a busy one."

Later that evening, Maray had arrived at the club at eight o'clock on the dot, thanks in part to Smitt's running over to pick her up. And just like the previous night, she was stunning.

This time she wore her hair bunched up into some sort of messy confection on the top of her head and was killing it in one of the Diane von Furstenberg wrap dresses I'd picked out for her. This one was a bright orange, and it hugged her curves just like I had the night before when I spooned her.

Best of all, she was beaming.

I greeted the night's players, and when their games kicked off, I worked my way over to Maray. I'd told myself I was going to resist talking to her until the end of the night, to remain 'professional.'

Fuck that.

Plus, I had something to give her.

"And what are you all smiles about?" I asked.

She organized her chips and logged into the club's system. "Well. Remember how you found me studying last night?"

I nodded. "Yeah, I do. And I remember how you were gone before I even got up."

She tossed her head back and laughed. "Yup, I did that, too. I had an exam to get to. But—I just got my grade, and guess what I got?"

I didn't have to guess. I knew.

I reached into my pocket. "Perfect timing, then. Congrats on your A," I said, handing her a small Tiffany box.

She gasped as I placed it in her hand. "Oh my god. I've never had anything from Tiffany. Thank you, Leo," she said, throwing her arms around my neck.

Yup, everyone looked our way. Ask me if I gave a shit. It was my club, after all.

"C'mon. Open it."

She tore at the little turquoise box, pulling out a sterling bangle that she slipped over her wrist.

"It's beautiful," she breathed. "Thank you."

I held her hand to see the bracelet.

The way she looked up at me with her wide eyes made me want to take her right there. In fact, if we hadn't had three games just underway, I might have spirited her back to my office so I could really show her how I felt.

Just then, my cell rang. It was Smitt.

"All right. Send them up."

The elevator doors opened and closed, and out stepped two of the Russian guys who ran card games across town. The ones who had issues with how we did business. They marched across the game room toward Maray and me, their slick hair and gold chains glistening in the bright lights, wearing pointy shoes, tight leather jackets, and ill-fitting trousers. They pulled themselves up to full height when they realized that both Maray and I were much taller than they.

"Hello, Leo. May we have a word with you?" the younger one asked.

"Of course. What can I do for you, gentlemen?"

They looked at Maray and then around the room, their tough-guy garb attracting more than a few curious looks.

"In your office, Leo?"

I considered it, then shook my head. "You can speak freely in front of my associate here."

They'd already been looking her up and down.

Her eyes widened and she turned back to the computer, clearly preferring *not* to hear what the Russians had come for.

"So be it, Leo," the older one said in stilted English. "We are here to talk to you about your lending practices."

I knew exactly why they were there, but I wasn't going to make it easy for them.

"I don't lend money. I don't know what you are talking about," I said innocently.

He smiled at me, two gold teeth standing out among the rest of his yellowed ones. "I will put it differently. Leo, when you extend credit to players, that's an unfair advantage."

I pretended to have an epiphany. "Oh, you're talking about credit. Okay. Well, that's not the same as loans. But if you guys choose to run your business differently than we do here, that's your problem. Players come to my club because they like how we run things. If you're losing business because of that, you need to run a better show."

"Leo, we can't get the high-roller players when they know they can just come over here and get credit if they come up short."

I wasn't sure how that was my problem to solve.

I shrugged. "Like I said, you can always change the way you do business. Join the twenty-first century."

I patted the younger one on the back. "If that's all you guys needed, let me show you out."

But he pushed my hand off. "We are warning you, Leo."

I sighed deeply and caught the eye of the security guy, who started heading our way.

My politeness quotient had just run out.

"Get the fuck out," I said low enough that the players wouldn't hear. "You will not *warn* me about anything. Ever. And if you show up at my club again, I'll have a few warnings for you."

The young guy frowned and reached for his inside pocket. But my guard grabbed them both by the upper arm before they could do anything and directed them toward the door.

I knew they wouldn't raise hell in front of my players, because they wanted these guys to someday be their players.

Yeah, good luck with that, dirtbags.

"Um, what was that?" Maray asked when they were out of earshot.

"Competition. They run their business badly and get mad they can't compete."

She shivered, even though the room was warm. "Ugh. They were so skeevy. And did you see how they were looking at me?" She fingered her bracelet.

"Yeah, I did. Sorry about that." I swung an arm

around her shoulders and looked over at the guys waiting for the elevator. Of course, they glowered back at me.

The older one narrowed his eyes and patted his pocket to let me know he had a gun.

Good for him. He'd just fucked with the wrong people.

CHAPTER 28

MARAY

HOLY CRAP. Leo had given me something from *Tiffany*. Like the Audrey Hepburn Tiffany. The one with the robin's-egg-blue boxes and little velvet pouches, which every girl in my sorority seemed to have at least one of sitting on top of her dresser.

And the bracelet. It was sterling silver, engraved with the words *Tiffany & Co*. I'd never been inside a Tiffany store, but I knew their stuff was very exclusive and expensive. Not to mention, beautiful and classic.

Leo got me a gift.

Holy shit.

I'd be lying if I didn't say my heart was fluttering— even though I knew I was stupid to get excited over a little bracelet. He probably gave stuff like that to women all the time. He could certainly afford it. But I was tickled nonetheless, if for no other reason than I could wear it in front of all my sorority sisters.

Of course, that wouldn't come without a bevy of predictable, nosy questions.

Shit. Maybe I'd just stuff it in my pocket before I went home. As it was, when I hadn't returned home the night before because I'd stayed over Leo's, and instead arrived in the morning, I'd gotten some looks from the girls. But I was rushing so fast that when I *did* return, my face must have screamed *leave me alone*.

And Vivian, the world's best roommate, didn't utter a word. She just smiled at me and asked if I wanted to go to breakfast at the dining hall.

I loved that girl.

Not only was I in a tizzy about getting my gift, but I was also unsure what to make of the strange incident with the unsavory Russian dudes. I wasn't positive, because I didn't normally hang out with thug types— scratch that, I *never* hung out with thug types—but it seemed they were threatening Leo and his whole operation.

Whatever they were up to, they were wasting their time. Anybody could see they didn't stand a chance against Leo. Nobody did. I mean, when push came to shove, Leo and his team would always come out on top. It's just the way they were. Some people were at the top of the food chain and gobbled those underneath them.

The Russians were going to learn that lesson the hard way, if they hadn't already.

I just hoped I wouldn't be around to see any of it.

It had been a full night of games at the club, and everyone was finally gone except Leo and me. He'd even sent the security guys home, and I hadn't seen Smitt in hours. That was a little out of the ordinary, but I was pretty sure I knew the reason why, and that excited me more than getting the bracelet. Even more than the hundred-dollar bills stuffed in the zippered pocket of my handbag.

Waiting for Leo to do whatever it was that he did in his office, I took a seat at a card table and messed around with one of the used decks Delphine had left behind. A new deck was opened before each game, to make sure no one could cheat. The more I read about poker, the more I realized the lengths some people went to in order to win. The schemes were downright insane, not limited to substituting decks with *very* slightly different sized cards indicating their value, which only the cheaters knew about.

Why play if you have to cheat? I didn't get it.

I spread some cards across the table and practiced my poker face, imagining what it would be like to sit with heavy hitters who were betting tens of thousands of dollars, people who won and lost that much in as much time as it took to play a hand. It was strangely exciting, even though I was pretending, sitting there all by myself. But I got a sense of the headiness of putting

MIKA LANE

it all on the line. The anticipation that came with the unknown was kind of sexy.

I should know. I was sitting there, twirling my new bracelet, knowing that I should have gone home to get a good night's sleep. But I couldn't. I wanted to see Leo. I wanted to know what he was going to do with me. And to me.

It had been so exciting, watching him work the room over the course of the night, making players feel like welcome and important guests. His hospitality was the perfect cover for the intended purpose of keeping a hawk eye on the games, I was learning, to make sure nothing was amiss.

You couldn't be too careful when so much money was at stake, I supposed.

"Hey, beautiful."

Why did that voice always make me jump?

I giggled to relieve some of my tension and turned to acknowledge Leo, who'd come up behind me. With his hands on my shoulders, he kissed my ear. I closed my eyes, shuddering in pleasure.

Clasping his fingers, I leaned my head back against him. I couldn't help it. I should have been protecting my heart, but at the moment he was too good to resist.

He led me out of my chair and took my wrist, the one with the new bracelet.

I held it out proudly. "It's beautiful, Leo," I said. "I just love it."

He gave me his devilish half-smile that made me

both want to tear my clothes off and go running in the opposite direction. Nothing good could come of this. But at the moment, it was as though my feet were cemented to the floor. I wasn't going anywhere except right into this man's arms.

He brushed his lips over the back of my hand, then turned it to place kisses in my palm. The scruff on his chin tickled my skin, and my stomach fluttered in anticipation of more.

What was it about him?

He wasn't my type, if I even had a type. Well, I guess I did. There was that frat boy, whom I'd set my sights on, who would really be perfect for me, at least on paper. He was good-looking, from a nice family, and had a solid future. And he wasn't involved in the marginally legal world of high-stakes card games or anything like it.

But when I thought about it, how fucking boring was that?

With my hands on either side of Leo's face, I brought my lips to his, first brushing mine back and forth, then flicking my tongue over his.

With big handfuls of my ass, he pulled me close, so close I could barely breathe, his cock hard and grinding. I so wanted to take his erection in my hand.

But I wasn't ready. Yet.

Hell if I knew what a guy like Leo was doing hanging out with me, but at that moment all I wanted to do was tear off my clothes and feel his muscular body between my legs. Taking matters into my own hands, I opened my wrap dress, and as soon as it tumbled off my shoulders, he yanked down the lace of my bra and closed in on one of my nipples. His facial hair grazed my heated flesh, and as he sucked harder, a lightning bolt of sensation fired, landing right between my legs.

I pushed his suit jacket off and to the floor and fumbled with the buttons on his starched shirt. Next, I reached for his belt and fly and grabbed his cock from a tangle of boxers and shirttails.

We were in the middle of the card room, and I didn't care.

In fact, I kind of liked it.

Running my grip along his erection from root to tip, I found my fingers barely stretched around him. A drop of precum wet my hand, and when I moved to taste it, he groaned and laid me back on the table. Slipping off my sheer panties, I was left naked save for my matching bra.

Even though we'd messed around, I'd never actually been this naked in front of him, and while I instinctively wanted to cover up, his eyes roved over me with such appreciation that I wanted him to see all of me.

I went to kick off my five-inch-high Louboutin sling-backs, but he stopped me.

"Keep them," he growled.

Well then.

He parted my knees, running his hand over my smooth pussy, pressing and massaging my hungry sex.

I thought I might scream.

"You like it, baby?" he asked hoarsely.

"Yeah," I whispered.

"Play with your tits. I want to see you play with your tits."

I unhooked my bra and chucked it aside with the rest of our clothes.

Leo sucked in his breath as I kneaded and pulled my nipples. God, I didn't think I'd ever felt sexier, this gorgeous man admiring me like he'd never seen a woman before. He lowered himself between my legs, never breaking our locked gaze. I reached for his hair, but he stopped me.

"Hands back on your tits."

Okay then.

He slipped a finger through my wet folds and pulling it to his mouth, tasted me with that half-grin on his face, the one that had made my knees weak and any coherent thought fly out the window since the first time I'd met him.

"Tastes so good," he murmured.

He licked me from ass to clit and back, throwing me into uncontrollable tremors, and groaned when he grabbed my thighs and yanked me toward him until my ass was hanging off the edge of the table.

"I want you to fuck me," I said.

He stopped and looked at me, tilting his head with a

scarily serious expression. Reaching into the pocket of the trousers strewn on the floor, he came back with a condom and sheathed himself.

"Guide me," he growled, ramming my knees into my chest.

I directed his cock to my opening, shimmying my hips just enough to fit him inside my entrance. He eased his head in and paused.

I squeezed my eyes and gasped. Fuck, he was big.

"You okay?" he asked.

I nodded, unable to speak.

Watching me, he inched inside until he was buried. His eyes fell closed as he groaned.

"Feels so fucking nice…" he said.

He thrust, slowly at first but picked up speed until all I could do was thrash my head back and forth and pound the table beneath me. He'd stretched me to my limits, but because he'd taken his time, any discomfort had vanished. Pleasure vibrated over me from my toes to the ends of every hair. My own eyes closed, and the rush of blood filled my ears. All I knew were the waves of orgasm crashing over me as I reached for Leo, kissing him while he emptied himself inside me.

We went back to his place just as we had the night before. It seemed a little less warm without Bathsheba, but I told myself it was good for him to be back with his real owner. I didn't have time for a dog, and neither did Leo.

And just like the night before, I slept a couple hours, then got up to study. I knew I wouldn't get by for long with so little sleep, but the semester was coming to a close and I was in the home stretch. I was putting the finishing touches on a paper I'd begun the week before, using the new computer Leo had gotten me, when he joined me in his office, yawning.

"Don't you ever sleep?" he asked.

I pulled his robe tightly around me in the chill of the wide-open loft. "Of course I do. But I'm just jamming to get this paper done. I've looked at it for so long and reread it so many times, I can't even tell if it makes sense anymore."

He held his hand out. "Print it out. I'll take a look."

"Really? You don't mind?"

He nodded. "Believe it or not, I was a finance major, too."

Now *that* nearly knocked me off my chair. I mean, I didn't know much about the guy, but I had a hard time picturing someone running poker games and threatening Russians going through the ropes of earning a finance degree.

I guess the surprise had been pretty obvious on my face because it took him only moments to call me out on it.

"For your information, I was an A student, myself."

Well, shit.

So I gave him my paper to mark up and went to make coffee, when my phone vibrated.

It was my mother calling, at the ungodly hour of four a.m. And what was even weirder was that my mom never called. She texted, because she knew that was my preference.

"Mom?" I said when I'd swiped my phone open.

Leo looked up from my paper.

"Sweetie, your father is in the hospital. You need to come, now."

My heart began to pound, and my hands shook so hard it was difficult to swipe my call closed.

"I... um... I need to—"

Leo set the paper aside and took hold of my arms. "What's wrong, Maray?"

I couldn't look at him. All I could see was my dad's face. Would I get there in time?

"Can I get a ride to Long Island?"

CHAPTER 29

MARAY

ONE HOUR later I was running through the halls of my town's hospital in Suffolk County. Leo had driven me himself, protesting when I asked him to just drop me at the door, but respecting my wishes to go in alone.

"I'm here, I'm here," I said, flying into my dad's room.

"Oh, sweetie," my mom said, taking me in her arms. We turned to look at my dad, hooked up to a bevy of machines that beeped and whirred. He had oxygen going up his nose and appeared to be sleeping. Or so I hoped.

"What happened? How bad is it?" I asked, running my hand through his thick salt-and-pepper hair.

He didn't stir.

Mom put her arm around me. "Heart attack. No

surprise there. But he'll most likely be fine, thank god," she whispered.

Even though it was far from the best of circumstances, it felt so good to be with my parents after the recent craziness in my life, that I began to shake with sobs. I laid my head on my dad's chest, and the tension and uncertainties that had made themselves at home burst out of me.

"Honey, honey..." my mom said, rubbing my back. "Dad will be okay. I know he will."

I nodded. "I... I know, Mom. I've just had a lot going on. It's so good to see you guys, even if dad is laid up." I sniffled and laughed.

"Well, how's the semester going? You texted me you got an A on your test, but how's everything else? And why are you so dressed up?"

Shit. I was wearing the clothes from the night before.

"Oh, I was out. You know. I had to dress up." Time to change the subject. "When will Dad get to come home?"

She ran her hand along the sheet covering his warm body and tried to stifle a yawn. "Soon. Couple days, I think."

"Mom, why don't you go home for a while? I can stay here with Dad. I'll take a little snooze in the chair right here."

After my mother left, I got a blanket from the nurse and nestled into the chair next to my dad's bed. I sent a message to my professor that I'd email her my paper later that day and closed my eyes holding his hand.

I think I'd been sleeping for several hours when my dad's stirring woke me up.

"Dad… Dad, it's me. How are you feeling?"

He looked around the room, confused, and then his gaze settled on me.

"Dad, it's me, Maray." I'd jumped out of the chair, hovering over him.

He took a deep breath and rolled his eyes. "I know it's you, Mar. I had a heart attack. I didn't lose my mind."

Okay. Dad was back.

I burst out laughing, and when I was done, the tears returned. It was bizarre to be zipping from one emotion to the next so quickly.

But nothing about my life had been normal lately.

"Hey, hey," my dad said. "I'm not dead yet."

That made me laugh. I reached for a tissue and dabbed my eyes.

"Good lord, Dad. You gave us all a scare."

He took a sip of the water I'd offered him. "Well, I know you can't wait for the huge inheritance you're going to get from me, but it doesn't look like you'll get it anytime soon."

We both laughed. As schoolteachers, there was no inheritance for my parents to leave behind. Which was fine with me. I wouldn't trade them for the world.

It was so freaking ironic that, as down-to-earth as

my parents were, I was immersed in a life where I'd actually let myself feel pressured to risk it all and steal a freaking handbag from Saks. And I was working at Leo's poker games wearing clothes probably worth more than everything in my mother's closet put together.

"Your mother told me you got an A on your exam."

I nodded. "I did. I'm so happy."

"I'm proud of you, ya know," he said, squeezing my fingers.

If he only knew...

"But," he continued, waving his finger at me, "I want to make sure you have fun. Life shouldn't be all hard work."

Where was he going with this?

"Mar, I don't want you to make the mistake I did."

"What? What do you mean, Dad?" I asked, terrified at what he might tell me.

He took a deep breath and looking around the room, searched for words. "I want you to follow your dreams."

"Are you saying you didn't follow *your* dreams?"

"Well, I did, sort of. I always wanted to be a teacher, and I wouldn't change a thing about my life, especially you and your mother. But, you know... things might have been a little different had your mother not gotten pregnant with you right after we graduated from college. I was all set to travel around the world for a year. But instead, we got married and had you."

I'd known that my dad's plans were interrupted when he knocked up my mom. But he'd never really talked about them until now.

"Sorry to mess things up for ya, Dad," I said with a laugh.

He play slapped my hand. "You know that's not what I mean. I just want you… to keep your eyes out for opportunities. Don't be so serious about life."

Wow. My dad had never talked to me that way before. I guess having a heart attack will do that to you.

"Mr. Stone."

I looked up to see Leo had joined us, having approached my father with his hand extended.

"Hello," my father said, reaching to shake.

What the fucking fuck?

Leo was here, meeting my father?

Okay. Life officially could not get any stranger.

"I'm Leo Borroni, Maray's boyfriend."

Thank god I'd been half-sitting on my dad's bed, because if I'd been standing I would have fallen over.

Leo was not only introducing himself to my father, but also claiming to be my *boyfriend*?

Shit. This was not part of the plan. Not that I had a plan.

Dad's head whipped in my direction. "Mar? You have a boyfriend?"

I wanted to kill Leo. Until he looked at me, that was.

Bastard. The good-looking bastard.

"Um, yeah, Dad. This is Leo."

"I know. He just introduced himself."

Right.

"Well, Mr. Stone, I just wanted to introduce myself before Maray and I drove back to the city."

Presumptuous jerk.

"I'm… I'm not sure I'm ready yet to leave, Leo—"

My dad waved his hand again. "Don't worry about me, sweetie. You need to get back to school. I'm gonna be fine. It was so good to see you and wake up to your beautiful face." He pulled me to him and kissed my cheek.

"I love you, Dad. So much."

He nodded. "Of course you do. I'm loveable."

I shook my head and laughed. "I'll call you later today. Give Mom my love when she gets here."

He waved at me as a nurse came into check on him. Leo took my hand, and we left.

"What the hell was that?" I snapped, pulling my hand back as soon as we were down the hall.

Leo stuffed his hands in his pockets and shrugged. With that damn half-smile. "I wanted to meet him. See the father behind my Maray."

My Maray?

Okay. I officially had nothing to say to that.

"Have a good day, Mr. Borroni," a pretty admin sitting behind a desk said as we were leaving the hospital.

"Um, what was that about?" I asked, not sure I really wanted to know.

"Oh, before I went upstairs, I paid your dad's medical bills."

"You what?"

"You heard me," he said, looking out the window. "I wanted to help."

No. Just no.

"That is bullshit. First, you say you're my boyfriend. Then, you pay my dad's bill? How am I supposed to explain this to my parents? And where do you get off, anyway?" I crossed my arms, watching the Long Island Expressway whizz past as we neared Manhattan.

"That is so... just so... presumptuous. Not to mention not true. You are not my boyfriend. My dad just had a freaking heart attack. I don't need this added bullshit right now."

"Look, Maray—"

I held my hand up like a *stop* sign. "No. I don't want to hear it."

I was done. Just done with this man. He'd turned my life upside down and was now dragging my parents into it.

I didn't give a shit if he turned me in to Saks for shoplifting. I'd take the punishment I deserved. I had to get my life back on track. I'd get a new job close to campus, keep my head down, study, and deal with my sorority sisters.

It was the only thing I *could* do.

CHAPTER 30

LEO

"I'M SORRY," I said.

In the back seat of the limo, as we neared Manhattan, Maray's head snapped in my direction, her mouth slightly open.

Yeah, I'd apologized. I think she was as shocked as I was.

She thought I'd gone too far. But what she didn't realize was that I didn't play by the rules everyone else did. And she lived in a rule-bound world. I was trying to shake her out of that. She didn't need the bullshit sorority world someone had convinced her she did. It was holding her back, extinguishing her fire.

"You're lucky to still have your parents. Mine are gone," I said.

"What happened to yours?" she asked. "You never tell me anything about yourself."

I realized how little she knew about me. It was how I preferred to keep things. Until I couldn't any longer.

"My dad disappeared when my twin brother and I were teenagers. And my mom was murdered. By a family friend."

Her mouth dropped open, as I knew it would. That was part of the reason I didn't like talking about myself. Half the stories I had to tell were so unbelievable they left people speechless.

And I didn't want anyone taking pity on me. Ever.

"Oh my god. I'm sorry."

I shrugged as Smitt navigated through hellish traffic. "Yeah. My father was a Las Vegas businessman—" I used air quotes around 'businessman,' "—and one day didn't come home from work."

I gave her the short story about my dad's business dealings in pawnshops and liquor stores in the seedy part of Vegas, and how just as my brother and I realized they were fronts for hiding large sums of money, he disappeared. That was when our family friend Sal took us under his wing, and indoctrinated us into the family 'business.'

The same man who, many years later, murdered our mother when she threatened to reveal their affair.

"After we found out about what Sal did, murdering my mom, I had to leave Vegas. I needed a fresh start. My twin brother, Luca, stayed."

Maray reached across the back seat and took my hand. "That's a crazy story. Did you ever find out what happened to your father?"

I shook my head. "No. But Luca and I have our suspicions."

I hadn't shared this with a single person since arriving in New York. Only Smitt knew, and that's because he'd been with my family since we'd grown up together. He'd been through it all with Luca and me, right by our sides.

"I was impressed by how quickly you ran to your father's side. He must be a good dad," I said.

I would have done the same, given the chance.

Maray's hand flew to cover her mouth, and she nodded. "He is. He's such a good guy. He and my mom were teachers. Salt of the earth people. They've sacrificed a lot for me to be where I am."

A sob escaped her mouth. "I don't deserve it. They should not be sacrificing anything for me. I'm such a… loser." She buried her face in her hands.

"Maray, we all make mistakes. It's how you get up on the other side of them that matters. You would not believe some of the things I've done."

Crap. Now why had I gone and said that? Opened a damn can of worms…

She looked up, ready to jump in the opening I'd given her. "Yeah? Well, what's your story?"

Might as well just get it over with. I didn't want to hide things from the woman.

"I… I lost my fiancée several years back in a car crash."

Maray gasped. "Oh my god."

And that wasn't even the worst of it.

"She was pregnant. We were going to have a baby."

Years later, I could still hardly speak those words. They say you get over a loss, even big losses. But that was bullshit. You didn't. Not ever.

If you're lucky, you could get up in the morning and go through the motions of having a normal life. But it will follow you, occasionally tap you on the shoulder when you're having a good day, and remind you of the worst thing that ever happened to you.

"Oh my god, Leo," Maray said, tears spilling down her cheeks. "I had no idea." She scooted over, reaching for my hand and resting her head on my shoulder.

And it felt damn good. I didn't let people comfort me. I was a cold-hearted bastard that way. But I knew Maray didn't feel sorry for me. She sensed my pain and understood it was mine to live with.

And now I felt a lump in my throat. I swallowed it away. I didn't cry. Ever. "I wanted to help with your dad the only way I knew how. I tend to do that. You know, open my wallet."

She reached for my face and turned me toward her. "Hey. I appreciate it. I'm sorry I got snippy. I was freaked-out by my dad's being in the hospital and all that stuff. It scared the shit out of me."

I smoothed my hand over her hair. "I know you were scared. I don't blame you."

I wished I could do more, but I just didn't know how. Even though I knew she was slowly but surely melting my cold fucking heart. The amazing thing was that there was no shortage of women who'd tried to do that in the past. None of them had succeeded.

But Maray was different—in so many ways. And now I felt shitty for making her do all her 'tasks' in the name of a bet. I was such a douchebag.

"Can you drop me at my dorm?"

"Of course." I leaned over the seat, issuing instructions to Smitt. "Are you going to be by the club tonight to work?

"Yeah. I want to turn in my paper to my professor and get a nap first. I'm so tired."

Just before we pulled up in front of her building, her phone rang.

"Hi, Mom, sorry I left before you got there. Yes, Dad met my um... friend, Leo. I know he said he was my boyfriend, but... Mom, I'm in the car with him right now. Can I call you later? Thanks. Hey, and how's Dad...?"

Maray continued to chat with her mother, so I scrolled through my phone when I realized I had several messages from the guys.

Looks like the Russians are really pissed at us.

When will you be back at the club? We need to meet ASAP.

Fucking Russians. Up to no good, as usual.

I should have known they wouldn't walk away quietly.

"Hey, man," Nico said, when I'd gotten back to the club.

"What's up with the Russians?" I asked, taking a seat on the sofa in his office.

He shook his head. "Same shit every new game in town pulls. They can't—or won't—extend credit, so their players come over to our club because we're easier to deal with."

"Never mind that our club is the fucking nicest one in town," Colt added as he walked into the room.

Dom joined us as Nico leaned forward on his desk. "One other thing, Leo."

"What?"

"One of them—I don't know which, I can't keep their names straight—was asking about Maray."

What the fuck.

"Seriously?" I asked. "What did they want?"

He shrugged. "I'm not entirely sure. I got the feeling they wanted to hire her away from here. You know, she's classy and beautiful. They need someone like that to shine up the place."

After our meeting, I stormed back to my office without a word. It was one thing for those bastards to stick their noses into our business.

But if they even looked at Maray again... well, things would turn real ugly, real fast.

CHAPTER 31

MARAY

"Look who's back."

Weeza padded down the hall toward me with Muk Luks on her feet and a trapper hat on her head. Why was she always dressed like she was going on an Arctic expedition?

"Hey, Weez," I said, brushing past her.

"Well," she called after me, "guess girl with the rich boyfriend is too busy to talk to us now."

At that, I stopped. "Weeza, my father just had a heart attack. So why don't you get off my back?"

Lulu and Aimee came flying out of their room. "Gosh, Mar. We didn't know. Will he be okay?"

Deep inhale. "Yes. At least I think so. He's still in the hospital on Long Island."

Weeza clumped up to me, walking awkwardly in

MIKA LANE

her heavy boots. "I'm sorry, Mar. I didn't know." She threw her arms around me.

"It's been stressful. Sorry for snapping."

"But seriously, what about this new guy?" she asked, as Lulu and Aimee inched closer, like hungry lions stalking their prey.

So much for concern about my dad.

But I had to hand it to the girls. They were about as transparent as they came. They didn't give a shit about me or my dad and didn't even bother to hide it. There was some sort of sick integrity in that kind of honesty.

"He's not my boyfriend. I'm just, um, doing some work for him. At his club."

The three girls all looked at each other, excitement gathering on their faces.

"A club? No way. You're working in a *club*?" Lulu asked.

Aimee clapped her hands and jumped up and down. "Oh my god. When can we go?"

"Guys, it's not that kind of club. I mean, it's not a dance club. It's a poker club."

Their faces fell just as Vivian's had when they realized my new job wasn't going to grant them access to anything they could possibly be interested in.

Weeza scratched under her trapper hat, a trickle of sweat running down her temple. "Whatever, Maray. Don't tell me you're not fucking that hot guy who keeps picking you up and dropping you off in that Town Car."

What was she doing, watching me out the window day and night? No wonder they all got such shit grades. They didn't go to class, and they didn't study, not that it would ever hold them back in life.

No, they were set for success, no matter how badly they screwed up. That's what privilege bought you.

Me, not so much.

"You know, Mar, men like that don't hang around girls like you if they're not getting some," Aimee said, pursing her lips and nodding.

She didn't really just say that, did she?

Would I be expelled for decking a fellow student?

I'd be the first to admit, most of my sorority sisters were what I called *alpha girls*. And I was the beta girl. Always second in line, always taking the back seat, and always subjugating my preferences to theirs. That included keeping my mouth shut when I wanted to say something that might tick someone off.

But that beta girl was evolving into something new. Exactly what, I wasn't sure, and while I knew I didn't want to become one of those alpha bitches, the days of my putting up with their crap were coming to an end.

I wasn't sure when it happened, or even when I realized it. Maybe it had been gradual. But between the shit I'd been through with Leo, from his crazy tasks, card club, and dirty lovemaking, to my dad getting sick, I was a different person.

So fuck them all.

"Ladies, I want to thank you for your interest in my

dad, and for your interest in my love life. But I am exhausted and am going into my room. Alone." I walked into my room and started to close the door.

But the alpha girls, as always, got the last word.

"Well, Maray. I guess that means you don't need my dress for the formal," Lulu said with a smirk.

Huh. Hadn't even thought of that. I hurried into my room and grabbed the fancy garment bag hanging in my closet.

"Here," I said, thrusting it at her. "You're right. I don't need it. Thanks anyway."

She caught it with both arms, her mouth hanging open at the indignity of having her beautiful dressed returned without adequate appreciation.

I might not have the same shit they did, but I had my goddamn self-respect.

I woke up groggy from a long nap to find a missed message from the mentor and advisor I'd been assigned when I'd been granted my scholarship. Henry Truitt was an old alum of the school, and with his generous donations, he'd created his own scholarship. I was one of the lucky recipients. As a result, he liked to be hands-on, among other things, to ensure we were *on the right track.*

Cripes, if he ever found out about the shit I'd been

up to in the past couple weeks… well, it wouldn't be pretty.

"Henry," I said, calling him right back. "I'm so sorry I missed your call." He'd always insisted I call him 'Henry,' even though he was old enough to be my grandfather.

I could just picture him in his library, with a fire roaring and a brandy in his hand, warm and cozy and believing all was right with the world.

Privilege. In spades.

I'd been invited to his home once, along with the other recipients of his scholarship and a few of the administrators who wanted to make sure he was kept very happy, at all times.

They weren't fools. It was a huge feather in their cap to benefit from the largesse of someone like Henry Truitt.

"Maray, my dear. I hope you're well," he said. I could hear him smiling.

He really was a sweet man.

"I am, I really am. Very busy. I took a new job."

Shit. Why did I say that? Now he'd want details.

"Oh really? No more bagels?" he asked.

I started pulling together an outfit for that night's work at the card club. I was probably working more than I should have been, but the money was so good. And what the hell, the semester was winding down, anyway.

And I had to admit, seeing Leo factored into the decision.

"Um, no, they closed up shop on short notice. It was very strange."

He puffed on something, I wasn't sure whether it was a pipe or cigar. "Where did you land, then?"

"At a club. A very nice club. They play poker games there."

Silence.

Uh-oh. Henry was big on propriety.

He cleared his throat. "You're not serious are you, Maray? You can't be working at a card club. You know what kind of people frequent places like that?"

Actually, I did.

"Henry, I get paid in tips, and I'm making enough that I might be able to move out of my sorority next semester."

I'd been playing with the idea of Vivian and I getting our own apartment near Washington Square. Something small and tidy and private, away from intrusive sorority girls. I was close to being done with them, and I knew by the time I did move out, well, I'd be lucky if I hadn't slugged one of them. It was like all the petty humiliations they'd caused me were suddenly piled too high to carry around any longer. I was staggering under their weight, and it was time to make a change.

"The sorority. But Maray, I advised you to *join* that sorority."

It was true. He had. Along with his advice had come assurances that if one were to *succeed in life*, one did in large part by associating with the *right people*.

Even if those people treated you like shit?

"I know, Henry, and I appreciate that. You know I do. But I'm finding that these people don't share my values. Nor do the people I meet through their social circles."

Might as well just lay it all on the line.

Did that mean I shared Leo's values? I wasn't so sure about that, either.

"Maray, I've guided you in such a way that sets you up for meeting the people who will be your friends for life, and who come from good families with strong connections that you will benefit from."

He obviously didn't know some of the bitches I did. Which one of my sorority sisters had said she hated her mother because she wouldn't pay for her to get *another* boob job? And hadn't one of them bragged about having stolen cash from her dad's safe just before she left for Spring Break, which, by the way, was already being paid for by her dad?

Nice people, for sure.

"Henry—"

"Look, Maray," he interrupted. "I had to beg and scrape for some of the opportunities you've been handed on a silver platter. And look where they've gotten me. I am living a life I never dreamed I would have. I started in the Bronx and made it to the Upper East Side."

And, there it was. Henry Truitt wanted to help people only if they wanted to be just like him.

"Don't throw all this away, Maray. You can write your own ticket," he said.

So far, the ticket I was writing didn't seem to be taking me anywhere I wanted to go.

CHAPTER 32

MARAY

I WAS RUNNING around at the formal before everyone arrived. Last minute details and all that.

"Maray, don't you look pretty tonight," Lulu and Aimee said in unison, eyeing my glittery halter dress with envy.

The one Leo had bought me. From Saks. That hugged my booty like there was no tomorrow.

"Guess that new job is paying you pretty well," Lulu said with a dig.

Why did they have to be that way?

"Thanks, guys. Hey, do you have a second to check the bar and make sure all the beer and wine was delivered?" I asked.

I knew giving them a task involving alcohol would be taken with utmost seriousness.

I'd corralled a bunch of girls from my floor to get to the formal early to take care of last-minute details. Promises of first dibs on the cute guys we'd invited was enough to motivate them to get off their asses and pitch in.

But I had to say, as crazy busy as my life had been lately, we were *ready*. The formal was going to be a hit, and all those girls who'd doubted me?

Well, they could suck it.

I'd tormented myself over the question of whether or not to invite Leo as my date. I knew if I did, it would attract unwanted attention. People would be talking about it for weeks to come. But I was tired of making decisions based on what others thought. This party was important to me, and if he were willing, I wanted him by my side.

We might have slept together, but we'd never discussed our status, aside from when he told my dad he was my boyfriend, which we both knew was not true. Not yet, anyway.

And did I really want that? To date a man who was essentially a mobster? I wasn't sure what that even meant.

But my work on the formal was turning out to be a success in the eyes of my sorority sisters because at exactly eight p.m. the guys from everybody's favorite fraternity began to flow through the door—handsome, young masters of the universe, their heads held high and their pockets stuffed with condoms. In a matter of seconds, the girls were all over them, and the late-night promise of blowjobs, and more, filled the air.

I kept one eye on the door in anticipation of Leo's arrival, which would be sure to turn heads, and twisted my new Tiffany bracelet on one wrist, and on the other, the old silver ID bracelet my parents had given me in middle school.

When I'd first arrived at the sorority, I'd been wearing the ID bracelet just like I had every day since I'd received it. But it took only a few whispers, snickers, and rolling eyes before I realized it was time to take it off.

Seemed ID bracelets were not considered cool anymore.

When I was getting ready for the party and came across it in the bottom of my jewelry box, I slipped it on. I hadn't worn it in years.

Fuck what they thought was cool.

I reached into the evening bag the personal shopper at Saks had chosen to go with my dress. I had no idea what had happened to the pink one I'd attempted to steal. Never saw it again. Didn't want to, either.

A sharp elbow nudged me in the ribs. "Hey, girl. Waiting for your guy?" It was Vivian, the only one I'd told that Leo was coming.

She was stunning as always, with her dark hair pressed in long, tight waves, and a strapless red dress that screamed old-school Hollywood. Not many people could pull off a look like that, but she did like a champ.

I was embarrassed I was being so transparent. "Whatever. If he shows, he shows. No big deal," I lied.

Yeah. I was sure Vivian bought that. My nonchalance wouldn't fool her in a hundred years.

"Oh, wait," she said, craning her neck toward the door, where the line of frat boys trying to get in was getting longer. The girls would be happy. Very happy. "I think I see him."

She was right. It would have been impossible to miss the most stunning and well-dressed man to probably ever walk through the doors of the art gallery where we were holding our event.

I stretched up to my full height and caught his eye. He smiled that half-smirk that made him so irresistible, and headed our way, bypassing the line where all the others obediently waited.

Interestingly, no one said a thing.

"Wow, look at you," he said, greeting me with a lush kiss on the mouth. "You are beyond stunning."

Vivian's mouth hung open and only closed when I introduced her.

"It's very nice to meet you," Leo said, all charm.

I hadn't been sure what it would be like to have him on my turf—in a setting that for once he wasn't in charge of. But I was getting the feeling that everywhere he went, he was more or less in charge.

That's an alpha, for you.

Leo, Vivian, and I worked our way over to the bar for a drink amidst the stares of everyone we passed, not to mention a few whispers and nudges.

It was to be expected, I supposed.

"Hey, Mar, aren't ya gonna introduce me to your friend here?" Aimee said, batting her eyes.

"I'm Leo." He extended his hand, and when Aimee didn't readily let it go after shaking, he subtly freed himself from her grip.

He was beginning to get the picture.

"You did a great job, baby," he said, steering me away from his adoring fans. "This gallery is very cool." He looked around, nodding.

"Leo, thank you for coming. I'm sure a college formal isn't exactly your idea of a good time."

He pulled me to him and kissed my head. "Are you crazy? I was invited by the most beautiful girl at the party. I'd be crazy to say no to that."

I felt a blush washing over my face. "Thanks. That's nice of you to say."

Hooking a finger under my chin, he tilted my face up toward his. "I didn't say it to be nice. I meant it. It's true. Look at you."

Our gazes locked, and it was like there was no one else in the room. I could no longer hear the DJ, nor the screeching laughter of girls vying for the attentions of rich frat boys. All I could hear was Leo's breathing as he leaned to kiss my hungry lips.

"What's this?" he asked, fingering my ID bracelet.

For a moment, I wished I hadn't worn it. It wasn't nearly dressy enough for the occasion, and I guess I was worried that he'd think I was a hick for wearing it, just like my sorority sisters had.

I tried to cover it. I'd put in in my purse later, as soon as no one was watching.

But Leo lifted my arm to get a closer look. "No way. I used to have one of these things. This is *awesome*," he said with a nostalgic nod.

"Oh, it's just a silly thing my parents gave me when I was a kid," I said, pulling my hand back.

But he didn't let it go.

"I love that you're wearing this. It's so old school. I wonder what happened to mine? I haven't seen it in years. Probably back in Vegas at my brother's house. Are you… trying to hide it or something?"

Busted.

I shrugged. "Oh, I wore it when I first arrived here at school, and my sorority sisters gave me some shit about it."

He shook his head. "Well, they're idiots. They don't know vintage when they see it." He glanced over his shoulder at them and shook his head, amused at the posturing going on.

I loved that Leo got the importance of something like an old bracelet. I was beginning to think I had more in common with him than the girls I'd been living with for the past couple years.

Wonder what Henry Truitt would say about that?

"Hey," he said, gesturing with his chin, "where does that door over there go?"

Before I could answer, he led me by the hand to the other side of the gallery and was slowly turning the knob on an unmarked door.

"Um, Leo, I don't think we're supposed to go back there—"

He smiled when the door opened. "It's not alarmed. C'mon," he said, pulling me in.

"I can't believe they didn't have this locked." I looked around at paintings and other art leaned up against the walls of somebody's office.

"Damn," Leo said. "This stuff is great. I should buy some for the club."

He settled into a cushy, velvet sofa. "And for you."

I turned to see if he was really serious, and as I did, he pulled me toward him. His gaze was locked with mine, and once again I was under his spell. No chance of escape.

Not that I would want to.

He inched up the sides of my dress until it was up to my thighs.

I looked down just as he reached under my dress, pulling my tiny G-string down to the floor and helping me step out of it.

With that out of the way, his hand wandered up my inner thigh, and when he reached my pussy, he ran a finger through its folds.

Which, of course, were soaking.

He growled. "Baby's all wet. You ready for me? You want some dick?"

I knew we shouldn't mess around in an office we weren't supposed to be in, but my hunger for Leo overrode any logic that might have interfered with our fun.

I gave him a small smile. "I'm ready. But are you?"

"C'mere and find out," he murmured, pulling me until I was straddling his legs. He dipped his hand in his coat pocket and produced a condom. Then, he reached between the two of us and opened his pants, pulling himself out of his boxers.

I stared at his erection, mesmerized.

"Don't be afraid. I won't hurt you," he teased with a wicked grin, sliding me forward on his lap after he'd sheathed himself.

He ran his length up and down my slit, spreading my moisture. "I'm gonna let you drive. I want to feel your pussy devour my dick."

That was all I needed. I lifted myself to notch him at my opening, and even though I should have taken my time, I slammed down on him until he was fully seated inside me.

And, oh the pure pleasure. He filled every bit of my sex and then some.

"Fuck, baby, you make me crazy." He lifted my dress to my waist so he could watch himself slide in and out. In the process, my bare ass was to the door. If anyone came in, that would be the first thing they'd see.

But instead of being nervous, I loved it.

Jesus, what was I turning into?

Burying my head into the crook of Leo's neck, I ground my hips, and my orgasm built, initially a small tingle between my legs, spreading like a wildfire through my stomach and to the ends of my limbs.

"I'm coming," I whispered, my head bucking as I slammed my hand on the sofa behind him.

"Yeah, baby. Come for me. Come on my cock."

As soon as I began to shudder and convulse, Leo let out a huge groan, one that would have been heard throughout the gallery if a DJ hadn't been blasting dance music.

"Fuckkkkkk..." he shouted and pulled me down tight on his cock. "Holy shit," he said, in between growls that were so fucking primitive and hot that they ignited another orgasm.

After we'd caught our breath, I reluctantly climbed off him and straightened my dress. I bent to pick up my thong, but he snatched it off the floor before I could.

"I'm keeping this little treat," he said, taking a deep whiff of it before stuffing it in his pocket.

All right, then.

I smoothed out my hair and swiped some fresh lipstick on.

Leo held out his hand for mine. "C'mon. Let's go show those bitches how cool ID bracelets are."

I laughed and followed him out, ignoring the looks that came our way for having disappeared for so long.

Henry Truitt's words rang in my head. "You have to be with the right people," he'd insisted.

Yeah, I got it. I think I was.

CHAPTER 33

LEO

"This is the last time, Leo. Seriously," Maray said.

My beautiful girl sat glaring at me, just before the night's card players were to arrive. Her long blonde hair was gathered into a braid and hung in front of her right shoulder, the perfect sweet contrast to the sleek black jumpsuit she wore.

"I understand, Maray. I really do."

She shifted uncomfortably. Even though we were clearly lovers now, having debuted at her formal dance, she was still nervous around me from time to time. And I knew that in this case, she was waiting for me to protest her quitting the club.

But I wasn't going to do that. As much as I loved having her there, and as much as the other employees

MIKA LANE

and players liked her, if it wasn't the place for her, I would respect that.

Although I didn't understand why someone would pass up the kind of money she was making, especially given how relatively easy the work was. I mean, yeah, there were occasional outbursts by the players, and thug Russians coming by trying to shake us down, but shit—that's why we had security.

I'd never put my girl in danger.

But in the end, it was her choice.

"Did something happen that led to this decision?" I asked.

She pressed her lips together and tried to look brave. "Yeah."

I was pretty sure I had an idea of what she was referring to.

"Tell me."

"Well, I was walking to class, and a car pulled up next to me. It was the Russians."

Was she fucking kidding?

I popped out of my seat, fists clenched, and walked over to her.

"Did they touch you? Did they do anything to you? Because if they did, I will kill them. All of them."

I could tell from the way her eyes widened that talking about killing anyone might have been too much information.

She shook her head and looked down at her hands. "No, not at all. But they asked me to come work for

252

them. Said they'd make it worth my while, whatever that meant. I said no thank you, but they were really persistent. Said they needed a classy lady like me, and why did I want to work for that dirtbag Borroni, anyway."

Christ. They were working it.

"When they finally got it through their heads that my answer was no, the guy doing all the talking asked me to dinner. I said no to that, too, and they followed me all the way to class. I was scared, Leo. I *am* scared. After this semester, I might just move back in with my parents. Get away from all this stuff."

Holy fucking shit. I knew how much school meant to Maray. I wouldn't let anyone take that away from her.

Smitt and I would deal with the Russians later. But at that moment, I had to reassure her.

I propped myself on the edge of my desk and took Maray's hands, trying to contain my rage. "I am sorry that happened. I don't blame you for being scared. I'm furious and wish you had called me the moment it happened. Those guys have crossed the line, and now they're fucked. Life as they know it is over."

She looked up at me with wide eyes. "What do you mean?"

I shook my head. "Don't worry about it. The less you know, the better. But I do have a proposition for you. It will keep you safe, whether you want to continue working here or not."

She scrunched her brow, confused. "What do you mean? What kind of proposition?"

I took a deep breath.

"I'd like you to move in with me. I will pay for your college, so you don't have to worry about scholarships or anything like that."

Her hand flew to cover her mouth, and she just stared at me.

"You okay, baby?" I asked.

She closed her eyes for a moment before she spoke. "Thank you. Thank you for your offer. It sounds wonderful, but—"

"But what?"

She took a deep breath. "Leo, I need to make my own way. I need to figure out who I am, where I'm going, and how I'm going to get there."

Damn. I think I liked her now more than ever. She had resolve. I loved that about her.

Shit. Did I just say *love*?

I pulled her to me for a lush kiss. If our guests weren't arriving, she'd be getting a lot more than a kiss from me.

And it seemed she felt the same with the way she melted into my arms, like she'd always been there, her mouth sexy and soft under mine.

"Ahem," a voice called from behind us. We both turned to find my business partners had joined us. We hadn't even noticed.

"Geez, guys," Colt said, "why don't you get a room?"

Dom and Nico laughed.

"Uh, guys, we do have a room. It's called my office, and it was private until you decided you were welcome in it."

Maray adjusted her hair and made to leave. "I need to get to my post. I can hear the players arriving."

She headed for the door, but not before she was stopped.

"Maray, congrats on completing your tasks," Nico said.

She whipped around. "What? I'm done?" She looked at me, and I nodded.

I'd wanted to discuss things with Maray in private and wished Nico had kept his big mouth shut.

"Yeah, you passed with flying colors. I have you to thank for earning me a nice chunk of change," he crowed.

But Maray didn't look happy. She wasn't one to be taunted.

"So glad I could make you some money, Nico," she said sarcastically. "As if you really needed more."

"Yeah, well, you lost me my money," Colt said, laughing.

"Well, maybe you shouldn't have bet against me." Squaring her shoulders, she walked right up to Colt and got in his face. "Maybe instead of using another human being for your personal entertainment, you could find a different way to get your kicks."

As if they hadn't already dug themselves in deeply

enough, Dom piped up. "Well, don't feel too bad, Maray. I broke even. So, I have nothing to complain about, thanks to you."

She glared at us all.

"You enjoy that little handbag you worked so hard for, why don't you," Nico teased.

Now he was going too far.

"I don't have the bag," she said.

Time to take the tension down a notch. "Yeah, guys, we—"

But Maray was jonesing for the last word. "Glad you creeps could have fun at my expense, but now that it's over, I have three words for you—*go fuck yourselves.*"

CHAPTER 34

MARAY

FINE. I was mad at the world. I was allowed to be in a shitty mood from time to time, wasn't I? Everyone else was. Why was I always expected to smile?

Because, as Henry Truitt would tell it, I was *going places*. And girls like me, who depended on the largesse of others, had to behave. We were permitted no bad days, no bitchy attitudes, and no snarky comments. Ever.

Obviously, that had worked really well for me so far.

As soon as my shift at the club was over and the last player had hit the road, I grabbed my jacket and escaped in the elevator before anyone saw me. My pockets were stuffed with hundred-dollar bills, which felt damn good, but the earlier mocking—or what I felt

was mocking, anyway—by Leo's asshole business partners had thrown my mood into a downward spiral.

And when I'd returned to my dorm, without so
much as a good night to Leo, my disposition grew even
more foul as I anticipated the stupid questions and
comments that were sure to come from the sorority
girls.

And, as usual, they did not disappoint.

"Holy shit, did your new guy get you that outfit?"

"Can I borrow it? *My* boobs would be able to fill it
out."

"Did you suck his dick yet? Because, let me tell you,
guys like him only wait for so long."

Really?

"You know, guys, someday, if you're lucky, a guy
will like you for who you are and not just whether you
swallow or not. Think about that."

I ducked into my room and locked the door, leaving
several shocked girls in the hallway. They probably all
hated me now. And I couldn't give a shit.

"Hey." Vivian stirred in her bed, where she'd been
reading.

"Oh my god, Viv. I didn't see you. You scared the
crap out of me."

I went to my closet and started stripping. All I could
think about was getting into the fleece jammies my
mom had gotten me at Walmart.

"How was work?" Vivian asked, sitting up on
her bed.

"Eh. It was fine, I guess. I told Leo it was my last day."

She slammed her hand on the bed. "Are you kidding? That's the easiest fucking money you'll ever make."

Easy money? She didn't know the half of it.

I sat on the edge of my bed, hugging a pillow to my chest. "Leo asked me to move in with him. And offered to pay for school."

Vivian's eyes widened, and her hand flew to her mouth. "Oh my god. He must really like you. You never let on that this was getting serious, Mar. What's going on?"

I shrugged and looked at my freshly manicured nails. I'd never been one for mani-pedis, and left that for the girls down the hall. But since I had to look nice for the club, and had plenty of extra cash, I'd started treating myself.

"I don't know. I mean, he's great and all—"

"Great?" Vivian asked, incredulous. "Great? He's not *great*, Mar, he's perfection on a stick."

I had to laugh at that. In fact, once I'd started I couldn't stop.

"*Perfection on a stick.* Where the hell did you come up with that one?" I asked, gasping for air.

She rolled her eyes. "C'mon. You know what I mean. He's gorgeous, polite to your friends, successful, generous…" She gestured toward the Tiffany bracelet on my wrist.

I didn't dare tell her he was also a mobster who grew up in an organized crime family, ran quasi-legal card games, was menaced by the Russian mafia, and made bets on girls like me who found themselves in a bind.

Yeah, nice guy.

And yet... I couldn't stop thinking about him. As different as we were from each other, the man really *saw* me for who I was.

And by some miracle, he still liked me. Cheesy ID bracelet, and all.

"Well, what did you tell him?" she asked, sitting on the edge of her bed.

To her dismay, I shook my head. "I said no, of course. I have to make my own way in life. I'm not taking the easy way out by relying on some guy."

"Okay. I get that, and I respect it. But is it really about not accepting help? I mean, look, you're on a scholarship, and beholden to Mr. Truitt. So you *do* accept help where you need it."

"Um, well..." I stammered.

She came over to my bed and sat next to me, putting her arm around my shoulders. "I'm not saying this to embarrass or humiliate you. You're my best friend. I guess I'm just pointing out that sometimes you seem like you don't believe you deserve the good things that happen to you."

"I don't get it."

"You're a good person, Mar. You deserve all the

good things that life has to offer. That may or may not include Leo, but you certainly deserve happiness, rather than going through life as if everything was an albatross around your neck."

Well, shit. And now, the tears were starting to come.

I stood. "You know what, Viv? I need to get some fresh air. I'm going for a walk around the block." I pulled on my down puffer and stuffed my phone in my pocket.

"I'll be right back," I said.

She walked me to the door. "Sure you don't want me to come with? It's pretty late."

"Nah. I'll stay under the streetlights."

One of the first things they'd taught us when we'd arrived at the school's urban campus was, when going out after dark, to stay on well-lit streets. It had served all of us well.

Vivian threw her arms around me and squeezed. "Love you, kiddo."

"Ditto," I said, just like I always did, and headed down the hall.

CHAPTER 35

MARAY

THE NIGHT AIR bit me with its cold, but it was also refreshing. I started my loop around the block, which would take ten minutes or less, when Leo called.

"Hey. You left without saying goodbye," he said after I'd swiped my phone open.

I sighed. "I know. I'm sorry. I'm just really tired and needed some time to myself."

"I hope you'll consider coming back to work here at the club. But hey, want to get together tomorrow? Lunch or something?"

My pulse quickened, like it always did with him. "Yeah, that would be great."

I was relieved he'd not given me a boatload of shit about bailing on the club. All I knew was that at that moment, I was confused as hell about everything.

"Okay, cool. Maybe we'll go to this new restaur—"

I hadn't really been paying attention to where I was walking, and just then, someone shoulder chucked me so hard my phone went flying out of my hand and skidded across the sidewalk. I managed to stay upright, but barely.

The odd thing was, how'd someone bump into me? The streets were nearly empty at the hour I was taking my walk.

"Hey! Excuse me. You almost knocked me over—" I yelled, scurrying for my phone.

I could hear Leo's faint voice coming from my phone on the ground. "Maray? What happened? Are you okay?"

But before I could get to the phone, there was a hand on my arm, and it squeezed into a tight grip. "Get in the car," a heavily accented male voice growled at me.

I looked around wildly, realizing I was the only person on the block. In my distraction, I'd walked down a side street that was not only dark, but also deserted.

Fucking idiot, I was.

"Let go of me," I yelled, hoping Leo would hear me, and that I might grab the attention of someone close by.

But of course he didn't let go of me and instead scooped up my phone, dropped it into his pocket, and began dragging me to the car.

"What's going on?" I screamed. "Get off me!" I tried swinging, but he had me tight. So I buckled my knees and dropped to the ground. He resorted to dragging me.

As soon as he'd pushed me in the car, I attempted to open the door on the opposite side. But, it was locked. Of course.

Because that's the kind of day I was having.

As soon as the man released my arm, I took a swing at him. But he blocked it, reaching behind my neck and slamming my face into the car seat.

"What... what are you doing? Please let me go..." I cried.

I kept squirming until he pressed my face so hard into the seat it was difficult to breathe.

Fuck. Was I going to die? Was this how it was going to end?

All I could think of was what it would do to my parents—

"Can you be calm, now?" the accented voice asked, as my phone started to ring in his pocket.

With my face pressed into the seat, I could only mumble, "Mmm hmm."

He let go of my head, and I lifted it an inch or two. The car pulled away from the curb, driving slowly.

I pressed myself up. Looking around the dark car, I realized that the guy who'd grabbed me, as well as the driver, were the Russians who'd been at Leo's, and who'd pulled up next to me on my way to class.

"What am I doing here? I don't have any money. And if this is about Leo's business, I don't know anything. I just keep track of the players, stuff like that. In fact, I just quit. I don't want to work there anymore."

He just stared at me with his ugly, amused face.

None of this would be happening if I hadn't stolen that fucking bag from Saks. One rash decision, and my whole life was turned upside down. No, worse than upside down. More like in complete ruins.

"Blindfold her," the guy in the front seat grunted.

I held my hands up. "No, really, that's not necessary," I pleaded.

But a lot of good it did me, because the guy in the back seat had something over my eyes in a matter of seconds.

"Sit still," he commanded. "It will make things easier for you."

What? Was he kidding? Kidnapping could be easy? I wanted to ask him what part of it would be easy, and when it would start, but I was pretty sure I wasn't going to like his answer.

"I was serious about Leo's card club. I don't have anything to do with it. I don't know any more than the little bit I do for him when he's holding a game."

"It's not what you know about his business," the guy from the front seat said. "It's what you *mean* to him."

Oh. Shit.

"Maray Stone, surely you know he is in love with you."

Holy fuck. These bastards knew my name.

And what had they just said about *love*?

"I… I don't understand," I said.

The car rounded a sharp turn and headed up what felt like a parking ramp.

"We don't care what you know about Leo's business. We know all we need to. What's important is how much you mean to him."

"In other words," the guy next to me said, "you are leverage. Very good leverage."

Oh. Shit. This was not good.

The car stopped and I reached for my blindfold.

"Do not remove that." He guided me out of the car.

I shuffled along slowly, afraid of tripping or bumping into something. We passed through a series of doors, all locked, I assumed, from the sound of turning keys.

"Put her in there," a new voice said, also heavily accented.

Fuck. If only I hadn't gone for that walk. I should have just stayed bundled up in bed, gabbing with Vivian. Speaking of which, she was going to be wondering where the hell I was since I was to be gone for only ten minutes or so. Leo, too, would know something was up. He'd be looking for me already.

But how would he find me?

I was lowered into a chair. A door closed and was locked from the outside.

"Hello?" I called.

No answer.

I lifted a corner of my blindfold and found I was alone, in a large storage closet with shelves of canned food and cooking equipment.

Was I in a restaurant?

I got up and tried the door even though I knew it was locked. I pressed my ear to it but could only hear muffled voices speaking what I was pretty sure was Russian.

Leo was not going to be happy about this. Not at all.

But he'd get me out. I knew he would.

Right?

I sat back down and rested my head against the closet wall, closing my eyes. It was late, probably one a.m. or so, but I couldn't be sure without my phone. I took slow, deep breaths to calm myself, but instead my mind revved into overdrive.

The first thought to bubble up was whether my dad was still in the hospital or not. Or if he was even okay.

Then, my conversation with Henry Truitt came to mind. His insistence rang hollow that everything I'd ever need *for the good life* was right before me. It struck me as even more ridiculous than when he'd first said it.

And Leo. The handsome, mysterious, tragic Leo. He'd started off as a bastard of epic proportions, coercing me into a game for the benefit of himself and his buddies. But he'd gradually softened my heart, I think, because I'd softened his. He'd been through some rough shit, losing his parents and then his fiancé and baby. I didn't know how you survived something like that—or if you even did.

I must have dozed off, because next I knew, one of the Russians was shaking me by the shoulder and telling me to put my blindfold back on.

"What's going on?" I asked, groggily.

He pulled me up by the arm. "Come. We're leaving."

"Wait," I said. "Where are we going? Please let me know what's happening."

He nodded at the blindfold. I took the hint and pulled it back over my eyes. I was in the dark again, stumbling and bumping into things.

It was all so fucking unbelievable. I mean, if a friend told me a story like mine, I'd either think she was crazy or pulling my leg.

Maybe shit like this went on in the world all the time, but it didn't happen to people like me. Or so I thought.

I hesitated, and the Russian pulled my arm harder.

Was this it? What this the end of my life? Tears filled my eyes as I thought about all the people I wouldn't see again.

We passed through several doors just as we had when we'd arrived, and I was helped into the back seat of a car. Against my will, small sobs began to escape my lips.

"Do not worry, Maray," the man sitting next to me said.

We must have pulled out of a parking garage,

because I could immediately see daylight around the edges of my blindfold. Christ, I'd been locked up all night.

I kept my hands in my lap because there really wasn't anything else to do, and just hung my head, the tears continuing to come. They weren't just because some Russian thugs thought they could use me to get to Leo, but because of everything, going all the way back to thinking that if I had the right evening bag at my formal, everything would be okay. Yeah, I was learning the values Henry Truitt wanted me to—go along to get along. But was that who I really was?

After what seemed like twenty minutes of driving around the city, turning more corners than I could count—most likely designed to throw me off—gravel crunched under the car's tires.

Why had we left the pavement?

When the car stopped, I was helped out, still blindfolded. I shivered in the cold wind. Thank god my hands were free because I could pull up the zipper on my coat.

"Sit here."

My arm was held as I was lowered to the ground and leaned against something hard. I put my hands out to touch the rocky surface the car had driven on. Where the fuck were we?

"Wait here. Do not remove the blindfold."

"Why? What's happening?" I asked.

But footsteps, crunching on the gravel, moved away

from me, until a car door opened and closed. The car screeched into motion and the sound of it faded to nothing.

"Hello?" I called.

I reached around and felt more jagged rocks, until I realized I was leaning against some sort of pillar or pole. The distant sounds of the city continued like the white noise they were for everyone who lived there—seagulls screeching over the waterways, taxi horns blaring, and the occasional overhead plane. But without being able to see, something about them was distinct. With no voices or footsteps, I realized I'd been dropped far away from any place that people frequented.

After another minute of relative silence, I scrunched down where I was sitting and lifted a corner of the blindfold. As I'd suspected, I was in some out-of-the-way lot. Where, I couldn't be sure. But when I was certain I was alone, I lifted the blindfold all the way. I was still wearing my fleece pajama bottoms from the night before, only now they were dirty. My ankles were cold because I'd not worn socks when I left for my walk, so I pulled my PJs down to cover them and stuffed my hands in my pockets. The gloves I'd worn were gone, as was my phone. But I still had my house keys.

Strange mercies.

I scanned to make sure no one was around and pushed myself to my feet. I was clearly somewhere on the East Side, although I couldn't see any street signs to know for sure.

I suddenly heard a car crunching on the gravel, so I ducked behind the large pole I'd been leaning against, my heart pounding in my chest. The tears started to fall again.

They'd come back for me.

I searched frantically for a place to hide. There was some sort of dilapidated shack just on the river's edge.

Could I make it there without being seen?

"Maray!" a familiar voice yelled.

Oh god. I sank to my knees, my shoulders shaking as I opened my mouth to release big, heaving sobs.

Crunching footsteps ran toward me. I looked up through tears and threw my arms around Leo's neck when he knelt before me.

"Baby, are you okay? Did they do anything to you?"

I cried loudly into Leo's chest as he stroked my hair and whispered in my ear.

More footsteps approached. "Is she okay, Leo?"

It was Smitt.

Leo hooked his finger under my chin and turned my face. "Are you okay?"

The fear in his eyes tore at my heart, and I nodded.

I was fine. At least I thought so.

CHAPTER 36

LEO

MARAY SEEMED NO WORSE for the wear, although she was in near hysterics when we found her.

Smitt had driven across town like the ballbuster he was, barely stopping for lights and pushing the limits of driving on city streets.

I loved that guy.

"There she is," I hollered as we'd pulled into the lot the Russians had directed us to.

She'd better fucking be there, was all I could think on the drive over.

Adrenaline slammed through my veins when I didn't see her at first. All kinds of thoughts raced through my mind—had the Russians led me on a wild goose chase? Or had some other thug gotten hold of her before I could get there? We weren't in the best part of town, and the isolated, deserted lot we'd been sent to could have been loaded with any manner of dirtbags.

When she peeked from behind a concrete piling, well, the relief that swept through me was palpable.

"I'm here, baby, I'm here," I'd said.

She'd collapsed into my arms, sobbing so hard I had to wait a moment before half-carrying, half-walking her to the car. Smitt waited for us behind the wheel, the whole time scanning for signs of an ambush. When I'd gotten her in the car and signaled for Smitt to get us the hell out of there, her head just fell against my shoulder. I pulled her to me, with her bloodshot eyes, runny nose, and matted hair. Poor thing looked like she'd been through the ringer.

Which I guess she had.

Fuck, I felt awful. None of this would have happened if not for me.

"You're safe now, Maray. Okay?"

She sniffed and nodded.

"Did anyone hurt you?" I asked.

She sighed and sat up. "No. Not at all. I was just scared."

I wove my fingers through hers and pulled her hand up to kiss it.

"I guess kidnapping by Russian thugs will do that," she said, half-laughing. "How... how did you find me?" she asked as Smitt steered the car back across town.

"The Russians told me where you were," I said.

She frowned. "Why would they do that?"

I looked out the window at the passing Manhattan streets. For all my complaints, I was going to miss the place.

"Because I met their demands."

It had been a no-brainer, really.

She slowly turned to me. "Demands? What were their demands?"

I hadn't wanted to get into it right off the bat, but there we were.

"I agreed to close up shop. Leave New York."

"You *what?*" she asked, her eyes wide.

"I'm closing the card club. If I hadn't…"

She gripped my arm with her free hand. "What? What would have happened?"

I took a deep breath. It sickened me to say the words. "They would have… killed you."

She gasped, covering her face with her hands. The severity of the situation was too much to take. "Pull over. Quick," she said, reaching for the handle on the car door.

Smitt maneuvered out of traffic just in time for Maray to get sick.

"Oh my god," she said, when she got back in. "Sorry."

"I'm the one who's sorry. This is all my fault." I squeezed my temples with my free hand, feeling like I'd aged ten years in the last few hours.

"What about your business partners?"

I shrugged. "They'll go do something else. Maybe come to Vegas with me. Maybe open a new club. Guys like us have options."

She shook her head. "You're giving up the club," she repeated, looking blankly out the car window.

I turned her to face me. "It was worth it, Maray. Giving up the club was small change to keep you safe."

It was one of the few worthwhile things I'd done in my life.

"I put you in danger. I'm not proud of that," I said.

She nodded slowly. "Yeah. But... you're leaving New York? That's... just incredible."

Was that sadness that washed over her face? I hoped it was, I had to admit. It might make the next part of our conversation go more to my liking.

"Maray, I've... made some mistakes in my life. Among the biggest was losing my fiancée and baby. It was my fault."

Even after a couple years, the words still stuck in my throat. But the truth was harsh. If I'd not had too much to drink that one night and insisted my fiancée drive home, she wouldn't have been killed by a truck running a red light. I would have been in the driver's seat, and would have born the brunt of an accident I ended up walking away from. I didn't know how many times I'd wished it had been me and not her. But that didn't change things.

And I had to live with that.

But I could also do things right, going forward. I'd

been waiting for the opportunity. Maybe I'd finally found it.

Never too late for redemption, and all that.

"I'm so sorry you have to live with that," she said. "What will you do? Where will you go?"

This was where the rubber would meet the road.

"I'm going back to Vegas."

Her mouth dropped open for a moment. "Seriously? Just like that? You're leaving the club *and* leaving town? Not standing up to those creeps?"

I laughed. "Oh, they're being taken care of, mark my words. In fact, several of them are probably taking their last breaths as we speak."

Horror crossed her face.

"I'm sorry, Maray, but that's the way it works in my world. It was one thing to mess with my business. I can tolerate that, to a point. But when they dragged you into it—well, there are no second chances. They went too far, and the price for that is steep. Those guys would have killed you without a second thought, and they'll do it to someone else if they aren't stopped."

She looked down at her hands, shaking her head.

I knew what she was thinking—*what the fuck am I doing hanging around people like this?* I'd be thinking that if I were she.

"So. Vegas. Wow," she murmured.

I took her hand. "Yeah. And I want you to come with me."

Her head snapped up, and she looked at me, frowning. "What? I can't do that. I have school, and—"

"I know. Of course you have school. But you can finish remotely. I told you I know people at the university. They will make the necessary arrangements."

But she just looked out the window. "No. I can't. Thank you for the offer. But I have to stay here. In New York."

She leaned over the seat. "Smitt, can you take me back to my dorm?"

He turned the car from the direction of my place, toward hers.

And I got it. She had her life. I had mine.

Ours had intersected for a short period of time. That's how it worked.

That's how it always worked.

CHAPTER 37

Maray

I WALKED STRAIGHT to my room with my head down, not in the mood for conversation with my sorority sisters or the nosy questions that always came my way. I wasn't sure whether Vivian had shared with them that I'd been missing all night, but I didn't want to risk it.

As if they couldn't tell something was up by the filthy mess I'd returned in.

I entered my room to find a relaxed Vivian watching a movie on her iPad.

"There you are," she said. "All good?"

"Um. I guess."

How much did she know?

"Leo called to tell me you wouldn't be back till morning."

Christ. More weirdness.

"*Leo* called you? How'd he get your number?"

She frowned. "I figured you gave it to him. You didn't?" She stood and walked toward me.

"No. No I did not."

But it didn't surprise me that he could get phone numbers when he wanted them. Christ, was there anything beyond his reach?

Well, me, for one.

"What the fuck happened? And by the way, you smell like a homeless person. Doesn't Leo have a bathroom?"

Ah, Vivian. Always so straightforward. But she was right, I was disgusting. Desperate for a shower, I started stripping and reached for my robe.

"When did he call you?" I asked.

"I'm not sure what time it was. I must have fallen asleep after you went for your walk, because when he called, it was still dark outside."

So much for her worrying herself to death over my whereabouts. She'd slept through the whole damn thing.

"But after I spoke with him, I tried to call you."

"Yeah. I no longer have a phone," I said, rolling my eyes. "Lost it."

Talk about adding insult to injury. Did the assholes really have to take my phone?

Vivian ran over to her desk. "Here. You can have my

old one. Just take it to your carrier and they'll hook you up."

A lump built in my throat. I might have been lamenting some of the bad choices I'd made in my life, and questioned some of the shit that had gone down lately, but did I really have the right to complain?

Leo had come to my rescue and was going to freaking kill the guys—if he hadn't already—who'd crossed him, and now Viv was giving me a phone. 'Course, I could afford one thanks to my earnings from the club, but I didn't need to tell her that.

"Oh my god, thank you," I said, starting to throw my arms around her.

"Wait," she said, holding up her hands like a *stop* sign. "Shower first, then we'll have our love fest."

"Fair enough. But first, tell me what Leo told you."

Had he told her *everything*? I somehow doubted it.

"He said you'd decided to stay over. He sounded almost... worried. Like something was wrong."

She sat up and looked at me. "*Was* something wrong? Did something happen?"

I was still in disbelief over all that had gone down, but I couldn't burden Vivian with the story. I just couldn't.

"Well, um, I think he loves me. But probably not. Not at all, actually. How ridiculous. Right?"

She threw a mean stink eye my way. "Um, no. Why is it ridiculous?"

Well, shit.

"I don't know. I mean, he's not in love with me. I'm a boring college student."

Vivian waved her arms around like a madwoman.

"Are you fucking kidding me? He's wild about you. Did you not see how he was looking at you during the formal? Everyone noticed. And if he wasn't interested, would he have called me, your roommate, to let me know what was up? God, Mar, I know you're brainy and stuff with your scholarship and straight A's, but damn, sometimes you really miss the boat."

"I don't know," I said, heading to the shower. "I have twenty minutes to get to class. We'll talk about this more later."

She laughed. "Sure thing, man killer."

Not surprisingly, staying awake during class was pure torture, but I managed to out of sheer terror of messing up my A average.

On the way home, I activated Vivian's phone and called my parents.

Dad answered. "Hey, Mar, how's my favorite girl? Haven't heard from you in a while."

My heart leapt at the sound of my dad's voice, and I fought back the tears that were threatening to give away my anxiety.

Um, you haven't heard from me because I was almost killed by some Russian thugs... but other than that, everything's great!

"You're home Dad, that's so awesome," I sputtered.

I heard my mom calling him in the background. "I

am happy to say I have a clean bill of health, although your mother is trying to ruin my life with healthy food." He lowered his voice. "Hey, maybe I can come into the city next week and we can go to that taqueria near you."

"Dad, um, I'm thinking of making some changes."

A chair squeaked in the background, and I knew he was settling at the kitchen table. "Want to tell me about them?"

"I… I feel like I've gotten off on the wrong path. You know, trying to please people who I maybe shouldn't be."

I told my dad an abbreviated story of how Leo and I had been seeing more of each other, and that he was leaving town.

And that I was thinking of going with him.

As soon as the words left my mouth, I could not believe I'd even uttered them. Yes, I'd given Leo a big *no* as soon as he'd run the idea by me, but to be honest, I think I knew even then that I'd say yes.

Dammit.

He was right. I could finish school anywhere. There wasn't much keeping me in New York—except the close proximity to my parents. Being far from them would be hard, there was no doubt about it. And I didn't know crap about Las Vegas.

What if I hated it?

Guess I'd cross that bridge if I came to it.

Dad cleared his throat just like he always did before

he was going to say something important. "I think you should go for it. You're young and you have a lot of life ahead of you. Try things. Experiment. You'll regret it if you don't. That's where I stand, and I'm pretty sure your mother would support whatever decision you make, as well."

I choked back a sob. I just couldn't hold the tears back any longer. "Thanks, Dad."

"You have a good head on your shoulders. You'll find your path. You just have to look around for it, first."

He was right.

"Thanks Dad. I love you."

"Love you too, Mar. Now, when can we get some tacos?"

In the cab over to Leo's office, I had a minute to gather my thoughts.

My benefactor, Henry Truitt, was not going to be happy. And my sorority sisters would think I was crazy —that was, until it dawned on them that it might be cool to know someone in Vegas.

Vivian would be happy for me. She was always happy.

And Leo—I needed to talk to Leo.

Who would have thought that when I stupidly decided to shoplift, my life would be turned upside down, and everything that happened to me in the following weeks would make me question who I was and where I was going?

So crazy.

"Hey," I said, walking into his office.

"Ah, best thing I've seen all day." He embraced me and placed a lush kiss on my lips. I sank into the chair opposite his desk because otherwise my knees would have given way. That's the effect the man had on me.

"You good? Something going on?" He closed his office door.

I took a deep breath. "A lot is going on. So much. Starting with the realization that I've been trying to impress some of the wrong people. Trying to fit into the wrong places."

He looked at me and just listened, not at all disturbed by my fumbling for words.

The man *got me*.

He knew I was going through something and was smart enough to let me think it through without getting all mansplain-y on me.

"Also... I have your money clip and wanted to return it to you."

He nodded. "I knew you had it."

"What—" I started to ask.

Of course he knew I had it. He knew fucking everything.

"Fine. The next thing is... I'm thinking about going to Vegas with you."

A smile exploded across his face, and he stood to pull me to my feet.

"That's awesome. So fucking awesome. I can't wait for you to meet my brother. I've already been on the phone with him discussing expanding the restaurant business he's building. And I'm thinking about getting a dog. One like Bathsheba. I'll need your help with him. Or her."

My eyes filled with tears for about the hundredth time that week, one of the strangest of my life. In the last twenty-four hours, I'd gone from being left in a gravel lot by kidnappers, to talking about moving across country and starting a new life. And getting a dog.

My heart melted at Leo's genuinely happy smile.

"Well, do you think you could use a finance person?" I asked.

He narrowed his eyes at me. "Hmmm. I'm sure we could, but with your criminal history, how do I know we can trust you?"

He was trying not to laugh. Jerk.

"Good point. Maybe you should take some more bets on me. See if I can handle the job. Keep my nose clean."

I pressed my lips to his. I just couldn't wait any longer. And if he were trying to say something—well, we'd have plenty of time to talk.

I didn't know what the hell picking up and leaving my life behind to go to Vegas was going to be like, but I was pretty confident that with Leo by my side, we'd figure our shit out.

In fact, you could bet on it.

Did you like *Nasty Bet*? Learn about the next book in The Vegas Mafia Chronicles, *Filthy Deal*

They're coming to get her. But they'll have to kill me first.

She saw something she should not have. Now her life is in danger.

That happens when you're in the wrong place at the wrong time.

And you get mixed up with the wrong man—me.
Her sister's missing, and she's next.
Not my problem, I always say.
But she was so… different.
So I made a deal to help.
And my deal was just as filthy as you'd think.

Download Filthy Deal

Find all Mika Lane books here

ABOUT THE AUTHOR

I'm contemporary romance author Mika Lane, and am all about bringing you sexy, sassy stories with imperfect heroines and the bad-a*s dudes they bring to their knees. And I have a special love for romance with multiple guys because why should we have to settle for just one hunky man?

Please join my Insider Group and be the first to hear about giveaways, sales, pre-orders, ARCs, and most importantly, a free sexy short story: http://mikalane.com/join-mailing-list/.

Writing has been a passion of mine since, well, forever (my first book was "The Day I Ate the Milkyway," a true fourth-grade masterpiece). These days, steamy romance, both dark and funny, gives purpose to my days and nights as I create worlds and characters who defy the imagination. I live in magical Northern California with my own handsome alpha dude, sometimes known as Mr. Mika Lane, and two devilish cats named Chuck and Murray. These three males also defy my imagination from time to time.

A lover of shiny things, I've been known to try new recipes on unsuspecting friends, find hiding places so I can read undisturbed, and spend my last dollar on a plane ticket somewhere.

Check out my latest series, The Men at Work Collection, about hot men and the professions that make them successful masters of the universe... and the women they love.

I'll always promise you a hot, sexy romp with kick-ass but imperfect heroines, and some version of a modern-day happily ever after.

I LOVE to hear from readers when I'm not dreaming up naughty tales to share. Join my Insider Group so we can get to know each other better http://mikalane.com/join-mailing-list, or contact me here: https://mikalane.com/contact.

xoxo

Love,

Mika

Made in the USA
Monee, IL
26 May 2023

34645824R10162